D1010920

I ♥ Oklahoma!

Also by Roy Scranton

Learning to Die in the Anthropocene

War Porn

We're Doomed, Now What?:
Essays on War and Climate Change

I ♥ Oklahoma!

Roy Scranton

Parts of this novel have been published in different form in *12th Street*, *LIT*, and *LVNG*.

Excerpt from "History and Biology in the Anthropocene: Problems of Scale, Problems of Value" by Julia Adeney Thomas, from *The American Historical Review* (2014) 119 (5): 1587-1607. Used by permission of Oxford University Press on behalf of the American Historical Society.

Published by
Soho Press, Inc.
853 Broadway
New York, NY 10003

Library of Congress Cataloging-in-Publication Data

Scranton, Roy, 1976– author.
I heart Oklahoma! / Roy Scranton.

ISBN 978-1-61695-938-8
eISBN 978-1-61695-939-5

I. Title
PS3619.C743 I25 2019 813'.6—dc23 2019003466

Interior design by Janine Agro, Soho Press, Inc.

Printed in the United States of America

10 9 8 7 6 5 4 3 2 1

For Ted and Sharon

"The stranger asks no greater glory till life is through than to spend one last minute in wilderness."

—CHARLIE STARKWEATHER

You lie, changin' shape, makin' promises. Get a new skin. Be a man. Be a woman. Start over. Yeah, start over. Wipe the slate clean and sing, sing in my ear like nothin' matters, walkin' down a dirt road and the night's as long as you are, one step after another leavin' someone I love and you won't shut up, dust god like memory, wind son rain, once upon a time I mighta got loose a you but now it's late and every night I lay down to hear you brushin' on the screen whisperin' swerve dappled monochrome down in the trees afeared or was it hopin' in the sudden plunge, your curves in my crotch, your hum in my jaw, like somehow if we'd just go on forever we'd never die.

So there's this guy and gal drivin' down the highway and maybe one picked t'other up or maybe they been lovers for years and now, only now, succumbin' to their feral dreams, can they see who at last they truly are. His name's Jack and her name's Jane and maybe they're alone or maybe they got someone else along, some witness to make it real, some audience, some third sex name Jesse, and they're cruisin' Nebraska and Oklahoma and Illinois and Texas and maybe they had good reasons for leavin', maybe they dropped a string of bodies behind 'em and robbed banks or maybe a dream died or a kid or maybe it's no more'n the fact that their lives failed to cohere wherever they was livin', or maybe they think it's passin' time, a holiday, maybe they think someday they'll pull up the exit ramp and come off the road back to the suburbs and their endless hours of windshield starin', gas-station midnight snacks, state park bathroom grottoes and back-seat sex, trash bag hangin' off the cigarette lighter, slow spin through the tuner at 2:00 a.m. catchin' voices like bugs writhin' in the mind a god, hot air blowin' through the window, Gideon Bibles, soft shoulders, mergin' and lanes endin' right, detours, orange caution loose gravel slow children yielding and no thru trucks, snowcapped mountains, cataract canyons, Ozarks and Ohios and Mississippis and Missouris will all come to a point on the horizon where it's the end of the line but no, no, you'll never stop they just think so, but still I pray maybe if I nail you bleedin' to the page you'll let me go

1. Holiday Road

Let us take a simple example. A man who travels by auto-
mobile to a distant place chooses his route from the highway
maps. Towns, lakes and mountains appear as obstacles to be
bypassed. The countryside is shaped and organized by the high-
way. Numerous signs and posters tell the traveler what to do
and think; they even request his attention to the beauties of
nature . . . Giant advertisements tell him when to stop and take
the pause that refreshes. And all this is indeed for his benefit,
safety and comfort; he receives what he wants . . . He will fare
best who follows its directions, subordinating his spontaneity
to the anonymous wisdom which ordered everything for him.
—Herbert Marcuse

"Reality has no audience—wait, tilt back, get more of the sky."

"I've got the sky. How much sky would you like?"

"I want him framed."

"He's framed. Fleet of foot and bearing his caduceus, he juts, chiseled limbs bursting from the façade, veiled in shifts of tattered steam, god of speed framed in blue."

"Okay. Just keep rolling." Jim started over. He could feel the flicker, the fortune in the cookie from lunch: Travel will bring you luck. Fuck, oh—"Reality has no audience, the world no eye. We are the warp and woof, the quanta of its waves, the thing itself: deep surface . . . Deep surface. We are the wave . . . Surface. Wave. Wave, surface." He exhaled sharply. "How's that sound?"

"I'm not the writer," Remy said, running the camera.

Jim turned and looked down the glowing red-eyed stream of fleeing UberATs. "Christ, I hope she says yes."

"You're going to pay her, right?"

"Yeah, sure. All artists fucking care about. Worse than Wall Street. You still rolling?"

"Yeah," Remy said.

"Nexus of roads, speed and space. Only in space do we become substantial, only in time do our lives take on meaning. Can you see yourself seeing? Can you look inside your eye?"

"Are you asking me?"

"No, keep rolling. Can you look inside the eye? Reality has no audience." Jim turned again and squatted on the sidewalk. Foot traffic split around the two, the click and slap of heel and sole, nowhere stares plugged into screens catching the blaze of towers burning down the West. "How was that? I just made that up. I just riffed off what I was thinking."

"I'm not the writer. Ask Suzie."

"She'd say it's pretentious. She'd say it's pretentious and what do I know from space and time."

"Is Carol coming?"

"Carol left ten days ago. Left a half carton of Silk."

"Oh, Jim. I'm sorry, I—"

"Fuck that. Been a long time coming. Some people can't fucking roll with the punches, y'know? Can't fucking adapt, adapt to change. Like fucking monkeys, adapt or die. She wants the old James, the golden days, but it's all space and time now."

"That's nice with the sun going down."

"You don't think it's too baroque?"

"It's all in the editing. Right now it looks pretty sublime."

"Sublime," Jim repeated, tasting it on his tongue. "I want medieval . . . You see that documentary about the bears?"

"Which one?"

"Fucking bears. It's just adaptation. These fucking polar bears are all gonna die because they have to swim all the fucking way out in the water to eat fish or baby seals or whatever and it's too far and all the ice is melting. The polar ice cap is melting. Imagine whiteness for miles, collapsing into encroaching black seas. So they have a choice, right, adapt or die, and they're gonna die because they're fucking bears. But that's the difference, see. We're not bears. We're like fucking not evolve maybe but whatever, pick up a stick, you know, duh duh duh. Ascend. Go west."

A bearded wreck swaddled in layers of sweatpant and plastic bag spun off the sidewalk into traffic shaking his paper cup, strips of foil glittering on his newsprint shawl like antimissile chaff. An UberAT swerved, honking, missed by inches. Jim watched, not quite tense but interested, wondering if he'd catch the whack and slam of body and street, hobo skull rebounding off yellow lines, the empty car's collision sirens keening. He thought to tell Remy to film it but no, wrong beginning. Wrong end. Why they do that, he half thought, on purpose? Or they so far gone past what's purpose, it isn't real? Everything meant but barely conscious, rationality of pure instinct. Sure, but which is more human, then, the wreck or the robot car? All secret agents of the brighter hive. Deep surface, Jim thought. That's good.

The man made it across the street and disappeared into the crowd. Another day, another failure to adapt. The smell of ash, charred flesh, and electrical, stone looming over shadowed warrens filled with particulate smoke. History's drone: a year is as a day.

"Good," Remy said, looking up from his crouch. "Shall we go?"

"Sure," Jim said.

Remy shut off the camera and disassembled the setup, unhooking the unit from its tripod mount, unplugging mikes, bagging gear.

"You want a drink?" Jim asked.

"Are you meeting Suzie?"

"Down in the East Village, one of those holdout trash bars from the nineties."

"I should drop the gear off."

"Well, if you're around."

Down the gulley of worn stoops and crumbling brown-stones bopped the gleaming machine, a chrome-detailed hydraulic import blasting Dominican rap, heavy beats in subtonal shudders making her knees vibrate, gut-thudding percussion wired to spat rhymes ending in long vowels and riding trilled errs like fast gears, East Coast style, a little reggaeton, a little islandy. If she was on her game she'd know what there was to know, but she'd been off lately, slippy, and she kept running into her ignorance like it was stalking her, pleading special intimacies. She'd open a new tab on her browser and there'd be this giant asshole, sucking the world inside.

And the solution was this? A field trip? She peeked out her window at the car going by below, the driver's arm out the window, the depleted afternoon light, brujas and abuelas on the stoops, then turned and looked at Steve the Cat looking back at her from under her bed.

Oh, Steve. She could text Cathy and be fairly certain she'd take okay care. It would be a favor owed, time expensed to Cathy's self-sniffing crises, but she was reliable. Yet more trauma for the *pobrecito gato*, already as New York neurotic as the pinched matrons of the parkside forts, those dowagers stumbling from affront to affront, Steve who was already

Krazy Kat, who lived under the bed and under the shelves and under the chair, Steve who did not like reggaeton.

This, though, here, right here, was what she loved, or so she told herself: the noise, the hum and thump, she never even had to put on music. There were those who needed quiet, to be wrapped in the numb hush of absorbed mind, but that was never Suzie's bag: she wrote in cafés, on the subway, in traffic, she wrote in the chatter of crossed wires, snatching bits of language and turning phrases from the air, pulling the true speech of men from the mouths of baristas, scripting it verbatim into fiction—she needed noise and pulse, tweets and hot takes—she thought herself a creature with antennae, a flesh-and-metal receiver, a time-traveling anthropologist making field recordings of the oversoul.

She drank her tea and looked at the screen. This, though . . . maybe not such a good idea.

It took about a day to get overwhelmed with sublet responses. She'd picked her fave by noon, a Finnish grad student researching American ethnonationalism. Suzie worried: Helsinki was a city, sure, but with reindeer, or without? Would Sinikka be bereft out here among the Dominicans and spend the first week huddled indoors, terrified of going out, her only sight of the city the peaks of its jagged skyline: the Chrysler and broken Empire, the more recent arrivistes at 432 Park and One57, the black mass of Trump Tower? I need to give her the address of the bodega, Suzie thought. For some reason the UberATs always got the street wrong. So there was that, and utilities, work, clear the calendar. Artforum owed her a check. Steve the Cat. Call Cathy.

All expenses, per diem, her own room, plus twenty-five

hundred up front and the same at the end, and cash, too, not even PayBits. A JetBlue ticket back from LA. Contractually obliged to two pages of dialogue each day on the road, plus forty pages beforehand to get them going, maybe a bonus for more. They'd share print rights, and she'd get an extra commission for any catalog accompanying the eventual show, if such a show were to happen. One-month commitment, though the plan was eighteen days, twenty max. It wasn't much, except it was, and it had potential, visibility, it could be—what?—not fun, what's fun? Fun was no longer a criterion, especially not with guys like Jim.

She could feel Steve watching her, prescient in his cat cynicism, already knowing she'd abandon him to her sublet's Finno-Ugric ministrations, already too disappointed to be sad, his Cheshire eyes gliding closed with shamed chagrin at the dumb vigor of the human species, the flailing wreckage these primates make of their lives.

Happy face. Out is back, away is forward. Life's not a luge but a gyre. That's the cost of something better than nine-to-five, anyway, the price of what you wanted, what you want, what did you want? Maybe you should have thought about that before the party ended, the lights dim in the dawn and the edge cutting back in through the haze you wallowed in, fondled by some jerk with too much bling and a bad, expensive haircut, the waves in the distance beyond the window you can't hear, rolling silently, the dawn silent, world silent, life silent and trapped in the spent mess of money, this jerk snuffling your hair, groping, waves rolling, was that what you'd had in mind? The lights so bright . . . Yet that wasn't even the nadir, tbh, especially once the bloom came off the barely legal, harder to maintain target weight, knowing too much to convincingly match the fresh new crop's blasted naïveté, as powders and pills came to occupy center mind, the account of a day tracked in altered states, so long until the next hit, so long, so long, but this one is the moment she's fixed on, fooling around with the heir to the fortune on his island, after the party, him grunting something Slavic, her putting herself through her paces.

Then there was a marriage. Now there's this.

She took a drink of tea. So long ago she counts it in lifetimes. What was important now was to focus on the way forward, do the work, put sentences together on pages and words in the mouths of imaginary people. Some days, though, she couldn't quite remember why this was so, crowded on the train watching the Hulu posters flicker, shoulders stooping, runway poise collapsing into the ruins of a former you, she couldn't really say what it was she thought she was doing, this bullshit sitting in classrooms listening to people talk, talk, *talk*. What a flagrant waste of human possibility.

Whatever. You gotta do something. When you're done maybe go out West and write a pilot. There are worse ways to make a living. Most important was to get free from this sense of cowering slippage, this feeling of having been pummeled by life, of looking for somewhere to ride out imminent storms. To find that thing, whatever they call it, where people look forward to stuff.

So the money's not great, but it's good enough, and it would be kind of like a vacation and maybe be a chance to get perspective, see the "big picture," visit that fantasyland called America, and maybe think things through in the slack hours spent rolling over interstate blacktop, maybe some feeling of freedom, a chance to wriggle out of the gray muck that lived inside, that shit her therapist called the past.

And Jim, she thought: Friend or foe? Was his fervor a phase, or a transition?

She shook her head, glancing at her pack of Parliaments silent on the windowsill. Not yet, she thought. Do your twenty lines.

Start over.

He took down his prep-school yearbook and flipped through, scanning for himself, letterman, salutatorian, track, lacrosse. Italian Club. Here's one, his senior picture, full-color gloss with a toothy sneer, and he remembered having his fingers up Becca Hunter the night before the shoot, huddled on the stairs at a party. She didn't want to talk to him after that, maybe because he told everyone he'd fucked her. He waved his hand under his nose now as if the scent might somehow have lasted.

Then he picked up his Pilot Super and inked himself out. Sweet chemical reek, permanent, permanent. He flipped through to Becca Hunter's picture, the girl standing smiling in front of a tree, and he can remember the contours of her body under his on the stairs. He licked the picture, but it just tasted like paper. Then he flipped back through to Debate, where he finds himself again, arrogant as ever, and blacks out his face and name. He goes through the whole thing, section by section. He forgot he was voted most likely to make and lose a billion dollars.

He closed the book and replaced it in the box where it had lain so long unseen beneath his boutonniere, his awards, his diplomas, his track letter, his framed first dollar on Wall Street that Carol made him take down because it was tacky. He imagined pouring lighter fluid on the box and burning it, putting it out on the curb for the homeless to pick through, or dumping it in the Hudson. Yet none of those fantasies satisfied; the past had a weight that wouldn't let him shrug it off so easy. Not without sacrifice. Not without blood.

He picked up his tumbler of scotch from the dresser and took a long swallow, gazing into the half-open, mostly empty wardrobe to his left, the hangers from which had hung his wife's assorted skins, her changes and masquerades. All her shoes were gone, but she'd left some dresses, underthings, and silky bits, took her makeup but left a scattering of crèmes and unguents. Just like Carol, to create categories of total control abutting categories of half assed, this just so, this whatever. Their marriage fit into the latter, he supposed, until it didn't anymore.

The half-empty bed, now huge and bodiless, still bore pockets of her scent, night-tortures uncovered in confusion and pique. The half-empty mirror on the wardrobe door no longer held her face, though it was her old black party dress he saw himself reflected standing in, fitting it awkwardly, the bust deflated but straining around his rib cage, material bunching at the hips (though not much, what with Carol's frankly somewhat androgynous figure), his lean, hairy runner's legs descending from the hem like hijacked limbs. Above the low neckline his shoulders erupted obscene, and his face gave the image its final lie, not improved by the lipstick and rouge he wore. Five o' clock stubble on a firm chin, craggy cheekbones, thick Adam's apple, his short, shaggy haircut. Still, his cock stirred as he stared.

He sat on the edge of the bed and lay back on their Icelandic eiderdown duvet, reached for the remote, and turned on the screen mounted over the dresser. He felt the inclination to be flying, not quite a wish, barely more than a velleity, but still a trace, settling into a first-class seat and feeling the ground fall away as the plane lifted, suddenly weightless, suddenly free, hours of blissfully empty time opening up, wispy white horizons, movies, sudoku, nothing, while at the journey's end the promise of unknown faces, a new city with all the same shops and restaurants, maybe you'd discover something important about yourself. Maybe you'd meet someone. He remembered his fingers up Becca Hunter and she was him, they were the same, his fingers inside himself, on a plane.

On the screen, Turkish F-16s bombed Saudi-backed Kurdish militants and fires raged across the Canadian taiga. He took another drink of scotch, dropped the remote, and reached behind him under his pillow for the revolver. The smooth, pitted walnut grip was cool and heavy in his hand: the Colt felt more like a chunk of rock than a machine, more like a club than a pistol. He swung it over his chest and opened the cylinder, counting: six copper-jacketed slugs fat as bees, big as fingers, waiting to go somewhere fast and bang. Then he rolled the cylinder closed and raised the weapon above his head.

It had cost him $94,785 cash at auction. It had belonged, apparently, to one William Van Wyck Reily, a young lieutenant in Custer's Seventh Cavalry. At the Little Bighorn, where Custer's riders fell and the dusty plain drank deep of their blood, an Arapaho named Waterman cut

Lieutenant Reily down, hacked off his fingers, and took his government-issued Colt. Later a Sioux named Two Moons took the weapon from Waterman. Later still, it wound up in the hands of the famous South Dakota collector Wendell Grangaard. Some suspected the weapon had been part of a cache of mementos buried with Two Moons, which had been stolen in 1960 when Two Moons's vault had been broken into. Others alleged the revolver was a fake. The weapon's provenance had been verified by Colt historian John Kopec, and the thing felt real, but Jim wasn't sure. Did it hum "Garryowen"? If so, he couldn't hear it. He'd spent almost as much trying to verify the weapon's history as he had on the weapon itself, but at the end of the day, all he had was a story.

He lowered the seven-and-a-half-inch-long barrel to his face, running the blued steel along his cheek. He licked the hole where the bullet came out, tasting metal and oil, the faint trace of cordite. Then he hitched Carol's dress up his thighs to his hips and rubbed the weapon against the taut satin of the panties he wore, a shiny purple G-string edged in lace. His cock strained against the fabric, calling out to the weapon in sympathy, aching for unification. He jammed the pistol grip between his thighs and rubbed it against his perineum.

It was time. He put his scotch on the nightstand and reached in the top drawer for the lube, then knelt on the bed so he could see himself sideways in the mirror over the dresser: the smear of red across his face, dress up over his hips, ass high in the air, face flushed. He slathered the Colt's barrel in lube, then slid the tip back between his cheeks, pushing the G-string aside. The metal was cool and firm against his sphincter. He breathed slow. Deep. He watched in the mirror as the barrel slid into him, long blue-black inches. The cold metal pressed against his skin, inside, outside, and his other hand went to his crotch. He imagined it was Suzie inside him, Suzie please, Suzie behind him and in him, Suzie fuck me, Suzie revolver, Suzie metal flesh, Suzie Two Moons Suzie Custer Suzie Trump, Suzie America, Suzie fucking Remy a great black wave.

"Nasty bitch," he muttered, coming.

Then, feeling guilty, he pushed himself off the bed, took a drink of scotch, and wiped the weapon clean. He slid out of his wet panties and washed himself, put away the revolver, and turned up the TV. He went out through the French doors into the living room. There was a great empty square on the wall where Carol's favorite painting had hung, an abstract thing in olive drab, hot salmon, and matte silver, the traces of which still played across his vision. It had been a good investment, ten years ago now, an early Keltie Ferris, and was almost as vivid in his memory as it had been in person. Like melted YouTube, sharply geometrical but spryly out of focus, a close encounter at the edge of visibility.

She let him keep his cowboy art, of course, the Tim Cox, Jack Sorenson, and Michael Swearngin, the imitation Remington. He'd had to fight for the Kehinde Wiley and Douglas Bourgeois, but they were his, his precious, his glowing black bodies shining out of wildly extravagant textures. In exchange, she took the Radcliffe Bailey and the Fahamu Pecou. He counted that a win, aesthetically and financially, yet it gave him little pleasure.

The maid had come in earlier and cleaned up all the molding takeout containers, the empty bottles, the dirty clothes, and he was struck anew as always with pleasure at the spacious emptiness of their apartment. His apartment, in point of fact, but he was willing to negotiate on that, too. Still. He looked out the window across the river at New Jersey, the lights on and off in the dark, America beginning there, a vast black continent sprawling to the ends of the earth, while the Hudson's water emptied into rising seas.

"And then we learned that becoming free from history was the same thing as destroying it," he said to himself, testing the words on the air, watching his reflection in the window.

He wondered if he had any coke left, then remembered he hadn't. Thought about taking an Adderall. Thought about going to bed. Took a drink of scotch.

He turned and shuffled down the hall to his studio, where he was greeted by the elaborate light show of his many blinking machines, processors and routers, external drives, his bank of flat black screens. He slumped into the captain's chair, tugging the dress down between his ass and the seat leather, and wiggled his mouse, bringing everything to life with a chitter and a hum. He opened up Final Cut Pro and Gmail and Twitter, scanning for new inputs: James, Please add me to your LinkedIn network; Limp Dickk, I have something for you!!!; *Artforum*; *e-flux*; Audible.com. Also real email from his lawyer, the curator at the Kitchen he'd emailed his latest Vimeo to three weeks ago, his mom, and Suzie. He would take them in order, breathing slow, his spent member slimy against his thighs. His lawyer was updating him on the divorce, Carol's most recent demands, the point in its life cycle the process had achieved, pupa, chrysalis, mutate, advising on "strategy" and "game plan" to handle this step, and the next, and the next. Rebuff, redirect, deflect, threaten nuclear, negotiate. Arctic sea ice collapse. UNHCR rep calls global refugee problem an unprecedented humanitarian crisis. Can China read your thoughts?

The curator turned him down, saying he liked the material, but the proposed project didn't currently meet their needs. This was the four-channel slo-mo pickup game he'd filmed, paying the lean black teens one hundred dollars each to let him set up his cameras around their game, plus the handheld, forty minutes of hard play strung out to four hours of slow dribbling and tossing, intercut with found black-and-white footage of birds flying over the city, overlaid with a mix of hard/soft ambient techno, somewhere between seapunk and witch house, fading in and out of recordings of Obama's speeches about Guantánamo played backward, the orange of the ball turned up so high it almost glowed, *Cage My Soul*, always one channel through the chain-link fence. Cultural imperialism, torture, race, rhizomatic distribution of the sensible, blah blah blah. Remy did some great shit on the handheld for that. These fucking shithead Eurotrash curators, they didn't want anything unless it was already famous or came from Yale, and they especially didn't want anything about actual people, real *stuff*, nothing about sports or fucking or work. They wanted war and dancing and Svalbard and media critique and the same old fucking vapid bullshit. But the real problem, he knew, was that he was a white man filming black men, which meant he was stealing, which was too close to the actual truth of the economic structures of the country to replicate within the ideological fantasy space they all agreed to call "art."

His mom wanted to know if he was okay, she hadn't heard from him in a while. She was having a fine summer at the house in Languedoc, pleasant enough though very hot, even in the mountains, even this early in the season. His brother had visited with his family. Was there any chance he'd make it out before fall?

Best for last.

He hovered the cursor arrow over the final message, testing his feelings. 360 Video from Nigeria. White Nationalist Intersectionality. Muslim Registry Bill Stuck in Committee. Do your employees think you're a good leader? Take this test and find out how. He could feel the very edges of hope and rage, the shoreline of an abyss, starry heavens shining in a black pool. All you need is a gun and a girl, a WingStreet Pizza Hut, traditional & bone out. All you need is sex and death and light. Was it still true that art something something something freedom? Or had we crossed the streams?

Well?

She said yes. She had conditions and reservations, but yes. She'd already started working on the script and had solved some of the logistical problems and she would go with him and Remy into the past and write the future. Freedom. Wilderness. MAGA.

He took a big drink of scotch, minimized Chrome, maximized the film he was editing. He worked late into the night, slicing, adjusting, making landscapes shake at precise particular rhythms, and all the while the vision in his mind was of a huge red car rolling fast down black road.

He unfolded the map, spreading the country wide across the table: America, broken by creases Jim tried to flatten with his hand, scribbled over in tiny coded ballpoint marginalia, random numbers, Greek letters, dollar signs, question marks, circles and triangles, routes highlighted in fluorescent coral pink and hazard orange. Suzie drew her rye back from under the flap and retracted her hands, thinking what the fuck—then, seeing her look reflected in the liquid warp of Jim's silver aviators, composing herself and pulling her face together, breathing, telling herself money in the bank.

"I found a 1971 Plymouth Valiant Scamp for only about fifteen thousand dollars," Jim said, holding the map down. "It's this ecstatic lime green. Really great. Bench seats, column shifter, crank windows, AM/FM, three-hundred-eighteen-inch cubic V8 engine, gigantic trunk. You gotta see it. You could cram a Girl Scout troop in that trunk. I also had AC installed, and a swivel mount in the ceiling for a second camera, so we can film constantly in addition to the handheld. We'll start as soon as I get in the car on Monday. Then I'll drive out to Brooklyn to pick you two up."

"Queens, actually," Suzie said, "but you don't need to come all the way out to Ridgewood. I'm sure we can take a train in, save an hour or two getting out."

"It takes how long it takes. I want the whole zoom, the sweep of urban decay, gentrification, and the BQE. I want Robert Moses, razor wire, and burning cars."

"Yeah, I can't really promise burning cars."

"I'll come get Remy in Crown Heights, then pick you up in Ridgewood, then we'll cross back over the Williamsburg Bridge to the Holland Tunnel."

"Why not just take the Verrazano?"

"Look, I want certain shots. I want the Jersey marshes and the terminals and I want the long shot of the south tip of the island. I want to cut that, see, with found footage from the same angle, old stuff, the towers, the absence, the empty sky, get it? Now you see me, now you don't, then we're off in the great wide open. My rough plan is to stab into the heart of Trump country, through Allentown and Harrisburg, riding 70 west more or less to St. Louis, then take 44 through Tulsa to Oklahoma City, 40 west to Albuquerque, where we'll hitch a sharp right north up I-25 through Denver all the way to Crow Agency, Montana, the site of the Battle of the Little Bighorn. Then we come back down, through Salt Lake, Provo, Las Vegas, and finally Los Angeles. Google says it's about forty-two hundred miles, so if we spend at least five hours a day serious driving, maybe more, we could do, say, three hundred fifty miles a day, which is twelve days in the car, leaving us six for sightseeing and rest. Then we wind up on the beach with Neil Young. I have a friend who has some oceanfront property out near Point Conception, he says he knows a good place to drive a car off a cliff."

"Which is probably illegal," Remy said.

"I don't mean go over with it. Block the gas pedal, light it on fire, slip it into drive, and whoosh. There it goes."

"Most definitely illegal," Remy said.

"It's the closing shot."

"After I'm on the plane, okay?" Suzie said. "I'm not interested in going to jail for felony littering."

Jim laughed, a bark pushed over the table like a fist. "Okay. So that's the big picture. Anybody have any requests? Diversions? Ideas? Places you'd like to go along the general route?"

"You want the script to start in the city?" Suzie asked. "By yourself? With us? You want some kinda Arthur Miller monologue get you going?"

Jim bit his tongue thoughtfully, looking creepy. "Good question . . . No. Let's start on the turnpike. Something inane."

"That's how I do."

Remy got up and moved the camera to take in a cross angle. Suzie felt him go behind her, but she kept her eyes on the maple table, the gray walls, the faux-distressed pictures of Belgium, the map. You'd think she'd be used to cameras, but this felt different, closer to reality TV, maybe, an all-the-time thing. More reality, maybe, or less. She couldn't tell yet.

"Where possible," Jim said, leaning over the map, highways shining in his silver lenses, "I'd like to take back roads. Old two-lane highways. The interstate's great and fast and boring, but I want a little variety. Especially out West. I want red canyons and blasting heat. I want white sand and rocket-blasted straightaways. Old diners. A sign swinging creaking in the wind and forlorn waitresses."

"Aw, gee, let me check my little book of clichés," Suzie said, picking up her rye. Remy huffed, somewhere between a chortle and a snort, then came back around and sat down.

"Precisely," Jim said. "All clichés. It's all about clichés. It's all about freedom and democracy and starting over and making a clean break and moving forward and making America great again. It's all fast cars and hot bitches and massive handguns. It's speed and death and sex. It's hitting the road and going west, Tom Joad and Jack Kerouac and the Beach Boys and John Wayne, James Dean, Lewis and fucking Clark. Bonnie and Clyde. Thelma and Louise. Mickey and Mallory. Charlie Starkweather driving through the Badlands of North Dakota. I want to inhabit the cliché so totally we're not even conscious of it anymore, we've gone beyond ironic, we no longer have the distance to judge or sneer or feel like it's something outside. I want to eat cheeseburgers and run from the cops. I want dark desert highways, cool wind in my hair. I want to live there. I want to be the dream. But this—" He smacked the table. "This is where you and Remy come in. You don't believe shit. You two fucking hipsters don't believe in anything. You're genderqueer post-racial cosmopolitan technocratic millennial ironists, cynical and smart and alienated and the only thing you believe in is abortion, democratic socialism, and Instagram. Whatever dialogue you write, Suzie, it won't be believing and it won't be living the dream. So that's one angle. The other's Remy, who's our floating eyeball. He's got the double consciousness and the double vision and the cyborg eye, he follows us and the car and the road and he sees what he sees. I'll set up shots and make certain decisions, but Remy . . . Remy's the nigger with his finger on the trigger."

"Jim, you know you can't say that," Remy said.

"I'm fucking quoting Snoop Dogg, dawg."

"Still not okay."

"Look," Jim said, losing his patience, "there's a triangulation. Like this. Here's me." He pulled a pen from his pocket and drew a dot, circling and circling until it took on weight, somewhere in Canada. "Here's you." He drew another, out Oklahoma way. "And here's Remy." He drew a third, Deep South Atlanta, then inked hard lines connecting all three, a giant Illuminati-blue triangle. "This area in the middle, that's the project. That's America. Contested space. A DMZ, fought over, emergent, reimagined. See? We're allies, we're coconspirators, we're partners in crime, but we're also antagonists, competitors, each pulling for our vision of the strict constructionist dream. I mean, I expect us to be contrary because I expect we'll be sick of each other in an hour. But there'll also be subterranean currents, a deeper agreement, a unified flow."

"Or you'll make one in the editing room," Suzie said. She still hadn't signed a contract. She could slam her rye, walk out, and go back to Steve and Ridgewood and her failed novel about Caril Fugate.

Jim leaned back. "Sure. It's my project, in the end. But for the trip, it's us. All three, full partners."

"What's the fucking point?" Suzie asked. "How is this not some high-art conceptualist retread of tired Tarantino bullshit?"

"It's a question of method and intent. First of all, I'm not remediating the old myths into new myths. I'm not trying to solve the problems the myths have created, or the problems the myths were created to solve. I want to explode the myths from inside. By reinhabiting the foam-space of the mytheme through the *Verfremdungseffekt* of digital images warped, broken, and melted beyond even post-avant sensibilities, I mean to reterritorialize the American dream as a body without organs, then burn it on the altar of negation. The problem isn't specific content: the problem is the dialectic itself."

"Sure," she said. "And you think breaking down narrative will have some kind of political effect?"

"It's not hashtag fucking Occupy MoMA," he said, snarling. "The point is total resistance at every level."

"So what . . . Godard by way of Trecartin?"

Jim slammed his fist on the table, loud enough that people looked. "She's great," he said to Remy. "Isn't she great?"

"She's pretty great," Remy said, smiling gently.

His grin was earnest, but his gray-green eyes seemed to empty the room. Suzie felt the urge to take his head against her chest and slowly unweave every Bantu knot in his hair. "You like cars?" she asked him.

Remy's smile shifted, the planes of his face realigning into an ambiguous, guarded half state. "Sure. Tech's cool. I suppose I don't often think about cars as such. Driverless cars, perhaps, as a form of artificial intelligence, but not as physical machines. They seem a bit old school."

"That's what I thought," she said, turning back to Jim. "That's my other question, Gene, is who the fuck cares? You and me, we're the last generation that maybe gives a shit about cars, and I don't even think we care that much. Him," she said, pointing at Remy, "and all them," she said, gesturing at the neodigitals slowly filling the room, their faces lit by handheld screens, "and anybody born after *Back to the Future Three*, their idea of freedom is whether they can change their gender pronouns on Yik Yak. Their whole idea of freedom is online, and even that's compromised by the internalized security state they've lived with basically their entire lives. So this whole mythic headspace you're talking about is really something only people even older than us have any solid connection with, and even for them it's a fucking ghost world. So this is what, an elegy? Some kind of MAGA nostalgia bullshit? I mean it just doesn't seem especially relevant."

"Yik Yak shut down like five years ago," Remy said.

Suzie glared at him. "Not the fucking point."

"Granted," Jim said. "That's what it looks like inside the bubble. We have our Uber-rats and TaskRabbit and Grubhub, meatspace never more than five miles from a Momofuku, unless you're roughing it someplace like Taos. But is the same thing true for kids growing up in, I don't know, Alabama? Ohio? Any of the other states that start with vowels? Yes, we think we come from the future, but they're all sliding into something else. You know what it's like to be a teenager in Missouri? You know what freedom is to them? Can you honestly tell me it's not a car?"

A knot began to form inside her, thinking back. "I don't know," she said, remembering saying goodbye to Oklahoma. "But they don't buy art."

"Fuck that," he said. "There's a place in America where

space still matters. There's a place in this country where a gun and a car mean as much as the flag, where the idea of freedom has to do with bodies, not just tweets and apps. A place where they watch the *The Fast and the Furious* and mean it. But I'm not from there. I'm from Connecticut. So I want to go there, wherever 'there' is, deep in the heart of it all, and make it make sense to me. I want to go where people believe the future means going back. I want to go where people believe in starting over. That's the point. I don't care who buys it. I have plenty of money. The only fucking thing I care about is the truth."

She laughed. "Okay," she said. "But I get to drive."

"I was planning on it."

"I also get to pick, when I'm driving, which road. Left or right."

"Of course. We'll discuss the route as we go."

"No, no, no, Gene, you're not hearing me. You say the trip is us, we're partners, fellow conspirators in total resistance or whatever, so let's be clear so we can put it on paper. If I get a wild hair up my ass we need to visit an old friend of mine in Cedar City and I'm driving, then we go to Cedar City."

"You know someone in Cedar City?"

"I got people all over."

"Sure. Sure. Yeah. If it's problematic, we'll discuss, but it's our trip, together, of course."

"No, Gene, you're still not listening. If it's our trip, it's *my* trip. I understand 'us.' I understand 'our.' I understand 'we.' I understand collectivity. But I need to know right now up front that this equitable shit isn't just talk. It's your money, it's your muscle car, it's your Final Cut Pro, so if you're really serious about it being *our* project, then I need fifty percent driving and total freedom to change course when I'm behind the wheel. In writing. I know for a fact you'd have not the slightest goddamn qualm about taking us on a two-day diarrhea tour through some Mexican narco transfer point if it so tantalized your rhizomatic muse, and this is a fact I accept about this whole ridiculous project. But we need to be clear"—she leaned in—"absolutely motherfucking clear, that the same rules apply for me. If I decide to drive to New Orleans, I drive to New Orleans. If we're equals, antagonists, whatever this bullshit is you're spouting, it's not some feminist-friendly palliative co-optation, all right? It's real."

"I'm extremely happy you're coming with us, Suzie," Jim said. "We'll get all that in writing for you."

Suzie shook her head. "I don't like you, Gene, and I don't trust you. I think you're a spoiled brat who never had to grow up, a thousand percent narcissist, jerk to the core, and whatever Damascene conversion you thought you had that turned you from just another Wall Street douche into a quote unquote so-called fucking video artist might have made you believe you had a soul to be saved, but you don't. You're just another shit with too much money, and this, all this, is just a long nervous breakdown. I'm happy to come along for the ride so long as I get paid, but we're not family."

"Fair enough," he said, grinning. His teeth and sunglasses shone in the darkness, a death's head in photonegative.

"Well, I feel tremendous spontaneous affection for you both," Remy said. "I think it's a dope project."

"Anything else?" Suzie asked.

"You tell me, pardner," said Jim.

"I think we're good," she said, checking her phone. "I need to go anyway. I'm meeting a friend to see Father John Misty. Email me the new contract and I'll get it back to you tomorrow." She belted the last of her rye and stood.

Jim rose and offered her his hand across the table. They shook, looking each other in the eye, then she was gone, leaving the trace of her scent, lemongrass spiked with the faint stain of burnt tobacco. Jim sat back and started folding the map.

"Shut off the camera."

They'd cut across lower Manhattan and come through the submarine-gray tunnel, lights overhead like smudged GloFish, thinking but only barely in the repressed hum how do they hold all that water up and what happens if something happens, smoke rolling into the tunnel, UberATs frozen, zombie swarm—escaping the city? taking it? the city itself boiling up around them?—slow but flowing out and up into the light of the mainland, the New World, American soil, blood and steel. A peeling billboard read JERSEY STRONG. On the radio, Terry Gross interviewed the author of *Truly, Madly, Virtually*, a memoir about falling in love with a DP. Remy filmed the tip of Manhattan just like Jim wanted, One World Trade, the Battery Park seawalls. A gull hooked and wheeled over Jersey City cranes.

"Brandon," Terry asked, "did you know she was digital when you started dating?"

"We were having such a great time," Brandon said, "it didn't seem to matter. The way I think about it, all of us are just collections of algorithms. We all have our patterns and programming and distributed cognition. We're *all* digital now. Beyond a certain level of complexity, who can say what's freedom and what's just a great app?"

The rhythm of high speed after the constriction of the tunnel lulled them into something almost Zen. I've made a gigantic mistake, Suzie thought, watching the signs for the turnpike.

"Should we start?" she asked, turning down the radio.

"Yeah, sure," Jim said.

"Okay. Let's do it, then. You start."

"Start what?"

"Say your line."

Jim angled his chin back toward his shoulder but kept his eyes on the road. "Remy," he said, "hand me my script?"

"You didn't memorize your lines," Suzie said.

Jim made a face.

"Okay, fine." Suzie said. "Your line's 'Was that our sign?'"

"All right," he said. "Was that our sign."

"It's your fucking movie, Gene."

"That's not what you say," Remy said. "Your line is 'What sign.'"

"I know my fucking lines, Remy, thank you."

"So say 'What sign,'" Jim said.

"I know what I say, Gene, I fucking wrote it. My point is it's a question. 'Was that our *sign?*' Like a question. You hear that? Our *siiiii-iign*. Rising intonation on the final *iiiiiign*. You were like, plop, 'sign,' I'm a robot. So, whatever. It's your movie. Proceed."

"I think they actually prefer the term 'digital person,'" Remy said.

"Robot, robot, robot," Suzie chanted.

"Look, Susan, my name's not fucking Gene and the cutesy bitchy act is already getting old, but fine. Fucking P.

T. Anderson here has *direction*, she wants a *read*, okay: Was that our *si-ign*?"

"What sign?"

"What the fuck do you mean what fucking sign?"

"That's my line. 'What sign?'"

"Fine. Okay. We'll do it again. Remy, the script."

"Here you go."

"All right. Mi-mi-mi. Hmmmmmmmm. Tip of the tongue, roof of the mouth, lips and the teeth."

"Yeah, yeah," Suzie said.

Jim pursed his lips, then pronounced: "To sit in solemn silence in a dull, dark dock, in a pestilential prison with a lifelong lock, awaiting the sensation of a short, sharp shock, from a cheap and chippy chopper on a big black block. Big black block. Short sharp shock. From a cheap and chippy chopper on a big black block."

"You done?" she asked.

"Was that our sign?" he said.

"What sign?"

"What the sign said? Was that us?"

"Not yet. These signs are just to get us ready. They're not the real signs yet."

"I was thinking about what she did."

"There's a pause there."

"What?"

"It says 'pause.' That means pause. You wait a beat, maybe longer. Pause."

"For Christ's sake," Jim said, slowing behind an unmarked black van.

"It's a flow, Gene," Suzie said. "It's the rhythm of language.

Back and forth. I know you do your rhythm in the editing room, but this is my stuff and the pace is important. Ta ta ti-ti ta. It's like Shakespeare. Listen to the rhythms."

"Shakespeare? Was that our sign?"

"I mean there's a rhythm to human speech. There's rhythms to the script, which I indicate with punctuation, ellipses, em dashes, commas, and directions. If it says 'pause,' pause. Let the silence fill up the space. Let us hear the hum, the low growl of the engine, the radio. Let the moment be itself as itself, framed time, let the environment play its appointed role. Otherwise it's all just fucking chatter."

"Got it," Jim said. He tapped the steering wheel. "My bad. Let's start over." He cleared his throat. "Ahem. *WAS* thaaaaat *ooouuur* SIIIIII-*heen*?"

"Now you're just being a dick."

Jim picked up the script and looked at it. "Ah, I believe your line is 'What sign?'"

"Fuck you."

"Well, let's take it again from the top. Was that our sign?"

"Fuck this. I should have known better. I knew you'd be like this."

"Like what?"

"For one, you don't memorize your lines; for two, you don't even read it; for three . . . for three, this is all about your fucking images, so I don't even know why I'm here. You don't care about words, about which words I'm using, how they go together in sentences and paragraphs, so what's the fucking point? Why not get a fucking robot to write it?"

"Digital person," Remy said from the back, insistent.

"Look," Jim said. "I'm not an actor. I do concepts. I'm

the guy behind the guy behind the camera. So I'm sorry that my line-reading skills are not up to whatever standard they're used to down at City College or wherever it is you take your master classes in rhythm and dialogue—"

"The New School."

"The New School. Whatever. The point is that I have neither the skills nor the interest for *performing* these lines in an actorly way. The text is the text and I respect that. I want your words. They matter to me. The rhythm. The punctuation. The semicolons and fucking subordinate clauses. Maybe part of the story can be me getting used to reading the lines, right, me learning to perform—adaptation, adjustment, chimpanzee piano. Blam! But we're not gonna get anywhere if you're expecting me to deliver, de novo, exquisite mimesis. I can't give you a fake real, Suzie, only the real fake." He snapped his fingers. "Shit, Remy, you getting this?"

"Audio's good. The ceiling cam's on the road, and I'm tracking the southern tip of the island with the handheld."

"So, shit," Jim said, smacking the wheel. "You see?"

The road surface changed and the ambient noise dropped an octave. Lady Liberty stood in the harbor, small and green, dwarfed by infrastructure.

"You were there," Suzie said.

"What? Where?"

"You were there. I just got it."

"I was where? What the fuck are you talking about?"

"When it happened. Your Damascene conversion."

"Sure," Jim said, reazling what she was looking at. "The greatest work of art possible in the history of the cosmos."

Pause.

"I was living off Washington Square," Suzie said. "I'd just gotten up. My roommate had brought home—"

"Can we not do this?"

"I'm—"

"Can we not do this fucking where-were-you bullshit? Because whatever you got, I can beat it. Unless you're actually a mangled corpse buried under a mound of slag heaped on Fresh Kills, unless you were physically inside the North Tower when the South Tower collapsed, unless you're a fucking firefighter with lung cancer who dragged some poor fuck from his doom, I can beat it and you can feel holy and proud and sad and American, and I can feel the same way I feel about it every fucking time I remember. Okay? Because what it was, the whole thing, was art. Living, breathing, dying human art, and it's more powerful than money and guns and feelings. That's the real deal and let me add this: I don't fucking care. None of it matters. It's all just dice, every—moment—rolling," Jim snapped his fingers once, twice, three times, "every moment totally random, accidental, it doesn't mean a thing, it doesn't mean a thing I'm breathing right now, today, this moment, fucking up your lines, nothing. Nothing! The only things that take on meaning, the only things that take on the weight of real fucking solid rock-hard substantial truth, are the things we destroy and say why."

"Jim, I'm sorry, I—"

"You know what, Suzie?" Jim turned to stare her down. "Nobody fucking asked you."

"Jim, the road," Remy said from the back.

Jim faced the road, swerved around a driverless semi. "I've just had it with the where-were-you bullshit, this obligatory performance of collective wounding—us and them, Christians and pagans, good and evil—it's all such bullshit. It's all random. All of it. Reality has no audience."

"Well, fuck, I—"

"Christ shit. First the lines, now the towers. What next? You gonna ask me about my mother? My divorce?"

"I wasn't—"

"You smoke, right? You got a smoke?"

Suzie dug in her Triple Canopy tote, pulled out her Parliaments, handed one to Jim, offered one to Remy, who declined, and took one herself. She lit Jim's smoke first, then her own. They cracked their windows. Remy coughed quietly. The car filled with smoke.

"Look," Suzie said, "if it's a—"

Remy touched her shoulder.

"Let's do the script," Jim said.

"Start over?"

"Yeah, start over. That's how we do."

"Ready whenever you are."

"Was that our sign?"

"What sign?"

"What the sign said. Was that us?"

"Not yet. These signs are just to get us ready. They're not the real signs yet."

Pause.

Freed from the city, something came loose, but she couldn't tell yet if it was good or bad, blockage clearing or maybe fine gears coming apart. Movement felt wild and portentous, lacking the grid to constrain it, and the lights out here went on forever. Rural America? One giant strip mall, more like, and some clot jarred awry was floating in its bloodstream, only a matter of time to see what kind of seizure it might cause.

She would have liked a balcony to smoke on, but the DoubleTree by Hilton was one of those box jobs, an irruption of prefab, poured concrete, and glass pushing up from the ground by the highway, square and gray and sealed against the road like it was quarantined, immunized against identity, pure shining globalization, from the blurry-eyed uniformed staff with their hidden tattoos to the screen bleeding Fox in the lobby. It might as well have been an airport. The room was "nice" but dull and shabby, and off in several less-than-interesting ways. The plastic cups were wrapped in plastic, and the hotel offered four Q-tips in a cardboard envelope as part of the complimentary grooming kit, but the single-serve non-Keurig coffee maker reeked of burning plastic, the overhead lights popped alarmingly, and the toilet seat was loose on its hinges. The giant screen worked, including seven channels of HBO, but none of the outlets on the desk did, so she had to plug her Mac in by the bed. The worst thing was that the only window coverings were thin, gauzy curtains—what seemed to be drapes were only narrow treatments, hanging fast on each side. Her third-floor view looked over the hotel's plant, a Howard Johnson, and a low-rising copse of Scotch pine; with the lights off, her room was flooded with yellow-pink illumination, as if she were sleeping inside an Easter egg. Were it not for the firm comfort of the mattress and the pleasure of clean sheets, she'd have preferred to deal with the mildew and bed hairs of the divey motor hotel down the way.

Lucky me, she thought, crossing the parking lot back to the Valiant, I don't have to face the moral quandaries of selling out—I got authenticity coming out my fucking ears. I already miss my cockroachy apartment and stolen mail. Let the Acela class sleep guilty in their white sheets, chum, I'm a proud and hardy working girl, rootstock of the nation, white, free, and twenty-one. She laughed. All this rude life, isn't this what you got away from? How come there's so much space out here, and why hasn't somebody filled it up yet?

Allentown, Shoemakersville, Hershey, Harrisburg.

Traffic droned on the Lincoln Highway. She leaned against the gold-reflecting green fender of the Valiant, feeling it heavy and metal and real against the abstract gray hotel and liquid road lights and looming geometry of the Alleghenies. She lit a Parliament and checked her phone, which, as per their contract, had been turned off all day long. Trash, trash, her boss wanted her to do some last-minute copyediting, three of her friends were going to see that new movie about the trans Nigerian refugee caught in Hurricane Wendy. The third act was supposed to be heartbreaking. She wondered if her Finnish subletter had arrived. She wondered how was Steve the Cat. She thought about texting Cathy to check, then let it go. She opened Facebook, then closed it. She thought about checking Instagram but didn't. She stuck her phone in her back pocket and watched the highway.

They got passed earlier by an open-carry motorcycle club, the Appalachian Vinlanders, a dozen low-rolling hogs growling by bearing lean, bearded men armed with AR-15s, shotguns, and pistols. Each leather jacket's back proclaimed the club's name in Gothic script, curling over an image of the Twin Towers rising out of flames above NEVER FORGET and 1488. Two of the men wore swastikas. Where were they going? What was this place? Scalp a fucker, what you think? They were silent for a moment watching the armed men pass—one turned and looked at them as he rolled alongside, flashed an "okay" hand sign with three fingers extended—then fell again to bickering, this time about whether "alt-right," "neo-Nazi," "white nationalist," or "white supremacist" was the appropriate term, or if they could say anything at all, since they didn't know who these specific guys were. "Maybe the swastikas are ironic," Jim said, stupidly contrarian.

All the snap and chatter, back pain, vigilantes—you must be low to find this worth 5K, or rather to find 5K worth this. Two more pages, two more pages. Trust the process, one word follows another, consciousness rushes in to fill the frame, narrative emerges, we can't help it. A and B but C then D. Or is it back to A? How can I be so tired just sitting in a car all day?

Five minutes from the battlefield. Beautifully appointed guest rooms focused on the business and leisure traveler. Each guest room features a refrigerator, microwave, coffee maker, hair dryer. A well-equipped work space includes two telephones, with two lines, complimentary Wi-Fi, ergonomic chair, large work desk, and adjustable lighting. Our fifty-five-inch HD televisions feature satellite selection.

More than anything suddenly out of the dark she wanted her coffee cup, her dirty table, Steve, and the new Nnedi Okorafor novel. Her cigarette smoke, the parking lot, half recalling the fragmented melody of something by Spoon— she thought she saw a ghost, but it was Remy drifting between the shrubberies. Maybe he is a ghost, she thought. Some kind of relief, then.

Remy was slim, slim hipped, hipster intellectual, and withdrawn. He'd undone his Bantu knots and wore his hair now in small dreads, she believed they were called brotherlocks, giving his head the likeness of a spiky ball stuck on the end of a long, wobbly stick. There was, she thought, something Eurotrash in his posture, something slack and hunched at the shoulders, an air of dignified defeat, perhaps, a postwar affect of monadic integrity sustained at no little cost amid the ruins of a betrayed civilization; she imagined he could have been a French Algerian Marxist poet, or maybe an Afro-Corsican post-structuralist philosopher. His face was yet more complicated, somewhere between DJ and mantis, with cheekbones dramatic and fragile as a lost hard drive, beautiful and damned, eyes the blue of dying glaciers. He never blinked, or at least she'd never seen him blink.

She heard him jingling keys as he walked up and watched a smile tremble along the edge of his mouth and disappear. That seemed right, that he should almost feel something, that his life should be composed of half states, like the cat in the box with the atoms and shit. He spent so much time behind the camera he didn't really seem to have a shape, existence-wise. Was he a full person, or just an assemblage? What did he really do for Jim? Was he gay or ace or weird or what? In it for the money? What kind of fucking name was Remy, anyway?

She remembered getting a transfer at a bus station one time somewhere in Europe with some boy. Neither of them spoke the language and there were many buses and they didn't know which was theirs and there were people going every which direction and it felt like they could get lost there, forever, like if they separated, the crowd would absorb them each into an alternating montage of dark streets and bands of beggars huddled around trash fires until finally they'd meet again, decades later, passing in the street without recognizing each other through their accumulated suffering and filth. She couldn't remember if they'd caught their bus or missed it. She couldn't even remember if the bus station had really happened or if it had been a dream she'd had or something she'd read or something she'd seen on a screen. Remy had something to do with it, though, she was sure, confident as a new ring tone.

"Do your eyes change color?" she asked.

"They do," he said. "What color are they now?"

"Dying glacier," she said.

"That sounds pretty."

"Yeah," she said, angling off his cool reply. "Earlier they were Ancient Mariner green."

"I'm getting an aquatic theme. You like swimming?"

She couldn't help but smile, just a little. "Swimming, drowning. It's complicated."

"So I gathered. Jim's gone to bed."

She had no idea what this signified.

He gestured lazily toward the Valiant. "Wanna vape some bud?"

She nodded. He unlocked the passenger door, then went around to the driver's side. They slid in and he turned on the radio. As they vaped, they caught the last few bars of "Don't Stop Believing," then station ID "WTPA 93.5 FM, Classic Rock That Really Rocks," then the chugging hook opening "Radar Love."

"Thanks," she said, handing back the vaporizer.

He took a hit and handed it back, then gripped the steering wheel with his long hands. "Pleasure," he said.

"I'm just, you know, the fucking driving," she said, slouching into the bench seat, "it's like I'm tired and cracked out at the same time. I can't just go to bed when I'm like this. The weed's perfect. Thanks."

"Yeah," he said, still staring at the windshield.

"No, it's really good. I mean it. Thanks."

"Mm-hmm."

"What a day, huh? Those bikers?"

"I always find it strange leaving the city. I mean driving

away, actually physically crossing the boundary out into the
rest of America. I can board a plane and fly somewhere and
that feels fine, like I'm still in the same world, but to get in a
car and drive out of the metropolitan realm feels like exiting
secured space. It feels, I would say, like going back in time."

"I can see that," she said, blinking, trying to make him
blink along with her. "I grew up out here, not here but here,
so it feels personal. What's weird about it for me maybe
is the inside being outside, but different. Uncanny, you
know?"

"*Unheimlich*," Remy said with a perfect German accent.

"Yeah. Right. My uncanny inside. But mostly I'm just
complaining about the filming and putting up with Jim's
bullshit. I don't know if the money's worth it, to be honest.
What's his fucking deal?"

Remy tilted his hands side to side in the air like meters
wobbling. "Jim is Jim is Jim," he said. "We've been working
together for a long time now. He can be difficult, but . . .
But, Suzie, may I ask you a question?"

"Shoot," she said.

"Why are you here?" he asked, his dying-glacier eyes
upon her.

She was trying to remember the name of that cat. The
one in the box. "You mean existentially? Or, like, right here
now?"

"Right here now."

"I came out for a smoke, cowboy." She looked into his
weird unblinking melting-Arctic eyes that seemed to be
filming still, then took another hit off the vape. "What
about you?"

He clicked his tongue. "How shall I put it? Jim's a damaged rich white boy on a slow glide path to self-destruction, and he's also totally faking it. All of it. His mastery of the vocabulary of contemporary art is dubious at best and often outright laughable. Even after all these years, he still doesn't know how to act and talk like a professional artist, because he's not one. He's an outrider. A barbarian. He wasn't socialized in the proper programs, Wall Street and American heteropatriarchy seem to have crippled him in unrecoverable ways long before 9/11, and then there was the event—which I'm not going to talk about, because it's not mine. He's an aggressive, unbalanced, mildly malignant narcissist and probably what they used to call in polite society an extreme eccentric. Notwithstanding this, there is something—some Miltonic glimmer—something quote, unquote, real there. It's as if he were a normal, average, regular old American Joe who broke, literally cracked open, and now he's bleeding truth like Texas oil. There's something nasty and insane inside Jim because there's something nasty and insane inside America, and he sees it and owns it in a way that people inside the bubble reject. I want to understand what he sees."

"Insider outsider art," Suzie said, watching the headlights from the highway sweep reflected in the hotel windows.

"Something like that. I bring camera technique and a sympathetic sensibility, though we see things quite differently. I like what he does with his editing. He surprises me sometimes, which is a rare and beautiful thing. He surprises me . . . even frightens me a little, and I find working with him aesthetically rewarding. Which is why I'm here."

"Okay," Suzie said, "but can I ask you a question about race?"

"If you would like," Remy said.

"You're a weirdo," Suzie said, running her hand through her hair. "But my question is this. You're black. Don't you already understand what the fuck's wrong with America?"

Remy smiled ruefully. "I could see why you might say that. It's not an unusual view, though I don't find it particularly persuasive. I've lived with racism in the United States all my life, but I've lived in France and Germany, too, and seen how those countries are racist as well, if in different ways. I'll grant you that racism in America is an ugly thing, a kind of institutionalized stupidity, but it's not unique to this place nor is it the sum total of North American culture. Racism is deeply imbricated in every stratum of American life, but the puzzling, painful truth is that the madness of this country is way more than skin-deep: it's in the mind and soul. There's a con man's apocalypse burning in the heart of the American character, a huckster Götterdämmerung seeded in its changeling birth, acorn to its lynching tree. This is the New World, genocide and utopia and Black Friday, school shootings and the Oculus Rift. Race is part of that, but not the whole thing."

"Even with the bikers, Trump, all that shit?"

"Racism is a symptom of something deeper, more ineradicable. We'll never be a post-racial society—Obama was probably the high point of race relations in this country—but even if we somehow were, it wouldn't solve the puzzle."

Suzie peered at Remy, trying to locate his power source. "Huh. Okay. So are you two a thing?"

He looked confused. "What do you mean?"

"I mean beyond professionally. A thing. You and Jim. I mean is it complicated."

Remy laughed. "Are you asking if we're lovers?"

"Something along those lines."

"Well, Suzie, Jim's a man's man and Jim likes women. I'm more flexible in that regard, though I like women as well. I enjoy sex. I'd like to have sex with you. Now it's true, I can't deny, there is a certain homosocial, even homoerotic, shading to my relationship with Jim. It's somewhat as if he's my big brother. I look up to him in a certain way. I want to *be* him in a certain way. But there also exists hate and fear and resentment. I nurse secret desires to sabotage his work. Sometimes . . . Well, I suppose it is complicated."

"Sounds like it. Do you have any actual siblings?"

He shook his head. "Only child."

"And did you just make a pass at me?"

"In a glancing fashion. It's early, though, and I'm satisfied to let our undeniable mutual attraction hang in the air, something we can look at and think about, come back to in our off-hours. I find anticipation often increases the pleasure of fulfillment, and I'm in no hurry."

Suzie handed back the vaporizer. "I think I'm done with the weed for tonight."

"Pleased to be of service." He tapped his long fingers on the steering wheel. A Prius pulled up in front of the lobby. "So, Suzie, where are you from not here out here?"

She lit another Parliament and opened the window. Cool air rushed in, pine and ozone. "I's raised up in a land flat an' wasted as the fields of Hell," she said in a vague rural twang, "where zombies roam the strip malls an' the future ain't nuthin' but the past caved in on itself. Ou'chere where Hope was a good girl once but now she's hooked on fentanyl, Joy choked to death on her own vomit, and Courage beat his baby mama's skull in with a wrench. It's a place where dreams are stillborn—when they ain't been straight aborted—a holy kingdom where givin' up's the only thing that makes any damn sense in this here life. Country ruled by King TV and conspiracy radio, where the national dish is gas-station hot dogs and the national anthem 'We Can't Stop' . . . Why'nt you guess?"

"So many choices. Indiana?"

"Close, but not as cold in the winter," she said, reverting to her normal voice.

"Missouri?"

"Warmer. Let me give you a hint. It's where the wind comes sweeping down the plains."

"Ohhhhhh . . ."

"Mm-hmm."

". . . klahoma!"

"Very good," she said. "You win the prize."

"Excellent," he said. "Gas-station hot dog?"

"You want a hot dog?" she teased.

He grinned. "I do believe Jim was planning on going through Oklahoma City."

"It was on his mental-disequilibrium map, if I remember correctly."

"Where in Oklahoma?"

"Altus."

"I don't know Altus."

"Who ever really *knows* Altus? Anagram for 'a slut.' Altus Air Base, Ninety-Seventh Air Mobility Wing. I'm an air-force brat, so, technically, I'm *from* lots of places, but we wound up in Oklahoma, and that's where I left. We settled there when I was in junior high. My dad was a first sergeant, which is a pretty big deal in the air force. He's what they call a loadmaster, meaning he knew how to put stuff on airplanes, cargo and pallets and trucks and even tanks. Very organized, very by the book, and his whole life revolved around training and military discipline and technical precision. So you see where this is going: he was a controlling patriarchal dick, and I grew up a trashy punk-rock rebel. I also happened to be great at standardized tests, a straight-A student, and National Merit Scholar, so that was my escape hatch. We fought a lot my senior year over where I'd go to college, but I wore them down and eventu-ally they agreed to let me go to NYU. Never looked back. It feels so long ago now, it's hard to make sense of who I was then, how young I was. I can't believe how fucking *hopeful* everything seemed. Like all I needed to do was get to New York and I'd emerge reborn, a whole new consciousness, in a radically new world. Everything was supposed to be different."

"Is it not?"

"Yeah, but through a mirror, darkly. That fall was 9/11. The spring of 2002 I started modeling, then dropped out of school, and now I'm here."

"You go back to Oklahoma much?"

"After the attacks, my dad wanted me to transfer to University of Oklahoma so I'd be closer, or at least go somewhere southerly, Rice maybe or Wash U, but I put my foot down. When I told him I was staying in New York no matter what, he said. 'That dog don't hunt.' He just kept repeating it. 'That dog don't hunt, Suzanne. That dog don't hunt.' He was terrified I'd get raped and murdered by jihadis, so he told me they weren't paying for any more school if I stayed. That's the last time we talked, and I got no plans to see them now. Jimbo wants to drive through Oklahoma, that's peachy keen, but there will be no happy reunions for the Calder family."

"I see."

"*Et toi,* Remy?" Suzie said in cartoon French. "*D'où viens-tu?*"

"I 'come from all over' as well, in my way," he said, "though perhaps a different 'all over.' My father worked for CNN, my mother's a doctor. When I was very young, my father was posted to Paris, so we all went along, and I more or less grew up there, though we came back to the States fairly regularly. My mother wasn't able to work as a physician in France, but she got a job with Médecins Sans Frontières, and I traveled with her now and again to Africa. When I was in high school we moved to Brussels. I went to school at Wesleyan, like my parents, premed, but then became obsessed with Alexander von Humboldt and spent a year in Berlin—which seemed a great rebellion, in its way, given my parents' Francophilia and my father's Jewish heritage—but they were very supportive, of course. In any case, it was in Berlin that I fell in love with German cinema and film in general, and when I came back to Wesleyan the next fall I changed majors. Then I got an MFA at CalArts, worked in Hollywood for a few years, and subsequently moved to Brooklyn."

While he talked, Suzie imagined taking his bottom lip in her teeth, and the image warmed her. Probably a bad idea, she thought, which didn't diminish its appeal. "You're cute," she said.

He smiled at her. "*Et vous,* Suzanne."

Then Suzie dropped her cigarette butt out the window, put her hand on Remy's knee. She watched him watch her, unblinking, as she leaned in, shifting in her seat, laying one hand on his delicate cheek and sliding the other up his thigh.

She looked down at the V-neck of his T-shirt. "I think I need some help," she said.

Horses in a field, black eyes staring, red dust rising round hooves.

Heaving to her feet at the knock, she fumbled her sleep mask off, glasses on, panicked at the strangeness of the room, whose room, when did she get a TV? Gray light poured in through the gauzy curtains and turned everything felt, as if the room were a Joseph Beuys.

"Yeah," she said, "just a minute."

"Get up," she heard Dad shout.

Thoughts connected by the most tenuous filaments, separated by yards of bunched cotton, pulled slow through rusted subterranean pipe. Road. Movie. Remy. The fuck's wrong with her? Every goddamn time.

"I'm up," she shouted. Her pants? Where pants?

"Time's a wastin'," Jim shouted through the door.

"Hold the fuck on!" A dark splotch on the carpet resolved into jeans and she tugged them on, stumbling toward the door, catching a look in the mirror, the puffy-eyed, slack-cheeked face of lo, how the mighty have fallen. You look like ass, Princess.

She swung the door open and leaned against it, glaring at Jim standing there in his mirrored aviators. "The fuck's on fire, Gene?"

"Morning, sunshine," he said, nearly chirping. "It's eight o'clock. We need to get moving so we can hit the battlefield. Up late working on your pages?"

"Yeah," she said, nodding, "sure, but then, you know, *Inception 2* was on HBO and I just can't resist Leo."

"Remy and I are going down to breakfast. We're gonna leave in like half an hour. That work for you?"

"Yeah, yeah. Good to hook. Save me a bagel, will ya?"

"Don't be late!" Jim said, grinning.

She closed the door. Thankfully, there wasn't much to pack, and also thankfully, after leaving Remy, she'd come up and written her two pages and printed them on the mini-printer Jim had brought along. She had a quick shower and tried to salvage a face, then said fuck it and threw on a pair of shades.

Jim and Remy sat watching CNN over breakfast wreckage, Froot Loops and apple cores and a pair of giant squid washed up on the beach in Indonesia. Two American special forces operatives killed in Sinaloa. Maverick and Goose looked up as she came in, and she realized they'd been talking about her: bros before hos. Remy's eyes, gray now in the milky light, never stopped filming.

"Saved you a bagel," Jim said.

"Where's the coffee?" she growled, squinting at two brats clambering over a chair at the next table and their dough-faced Oompa-Loompa ma blinking up in stunted hostility.

Remy gestured toward the breakfast bar. "Continental breakfast," he said. She could hear the scare quotes around "Continental."

She got her coffee and a bowl of Life, then came back

and sat, determined to play out her hand. "What's the rush, Gene? Playing soldier this morning?" She tore the plastic off her bagel and split the O with her thumbs, disturbed by how much the crust felt like a cheap PVC dildo. She watched an ad for paper towels—blue spillage, orgasm mouth—while she scraped butter across the plane of her bagel's face. She did not look at Remy. She did not even think of him. She refused to let his presence enter her consciousness.

"Gettysburg," Jim said. "The Battlefield. The blue and the gray, the Union and the Confederacy. Fourscore and seven years ago, something something something. I'm hoping for tourists, but mostly I just want the historical weight, the heaviness of the bloodstained ground. The Battlefield."

"The battlefield," she said, her voice flat. "Do you even know who fought at Gettysburg?"

"The North. And the South."

"I mean which generals, Gene."

"Robert E. Lee and Ulysses S. Grant. I don't care. Who cares?"

"Who won?"

"Easy," he said. "The North. No, wait. The South."

"The North won," Remy said, eating a Froot Loop. "Gettysburg is commonly recognized as the turning point of the war. Lee had advanced into Pennsylvania, hoping to take the war north to Harrisburg or even Philadelphia, but General Joseph Hooker and the Army of the Potomac blocked Lee's advance. Just a few days before the two armies met, Hooker tendered his resignation, and Lincoln gave General George Meade command over the Union forces. Lee advanced toward Gettysburg, hoping to engage and destroy the Army of the Potomac, but over three days of fierce fighting Meade's forces held. Around fifty thousand men died on both sides. Lee withdrew across the Potomac to Virginia, and the Union army took the offensive."

"The point is not particular narrative fact," Jim said, a twist in his lip. "It's the idea." He waved at the TV. "The point is you don't have to know. It's not about numbers and generals and all that fucking schoolbook bullshit. It's war. Blood. Violence and death and dramatic reversals. Every American knows Gettysburg and Lincoln freed the slaves and Lee was stabbed in the back. The point is the mythology."

She remembered the taste of Remy's skin, his long fingers bending and pressing, then the fumbling and choked excuses, backing out of the car, walking off leaving the door open behind her. "Tara," she said.

"Sherman's march to the sea," said Remy.

"Exactly," said Jim. "I'm not concerned with facts. I want the worship of mythical forms. I want fat tourists in cargo shorts and white sneakers kneeling at the bloody altar. I want people who have come to pray. The great forces that shake the world are not facts, not even ideas, but emotion, ignorant passion, blind aggression and terror and choked rage, superstition and racial hatred and witchcraft. I want to drink from the blood groove of American genocide."

"Well, you picked a good spot for it," Suzie said, gesturing with her coffee across the room, now filling with families in vacation gear microwaving egg, cheese, and sausage Jimmy Deans, pumping orange juice from the machine, peeling crinkly plastic off croissants, pouring GoLean into shiny disposable bowls, all of them half watching Jim from the corners of their eyes, alert to the atavistic rhythms of his rant, ready to align themselves and listening for the signal: Would this be the moment they were called to action? Had all their hours handgun training and filling out forms for concealed carry permits led them to this fateful crisis, here, now, in front of their families and the Hilton staff and all America, to rise as one nation and strike?

Terrorist tunnels had been discovered under the border wall, a lone shooter killed five at Spotify HQ, and Miley Cyrus announced she'd converted to Islam and would be making the hajj. "I think Sufism is the most beautiful idea in the world," she said.

"We should go," Jim said, his mirrored lenses reflecting bloat vigilantes angling shot lines.

"Let me finish my coffee," Suzie said. "What's the plan after Gettysburg?"

"The Battlefield."

"Whatever. After the battlefield."

"After the Battlefield, we head west. I'm hoping we can make it to New Castle tonight, home of the New Castle Fieldhouse: the largest high-school gymnasium in the world. On the way we do your pages."

"Okay."

"I was thinking you could write something not in the car. Like some dialogue at a rest stop or a gas station, maybe a restaurant. Like in the hotel."

"Like right now?" she asked.

"Yeah, like right now," he said.

"Well, I wrote this scene," she said. "Just like this. My words in your mouth."

Jim frowned. "I mean something dramatic. Engaging. It's important to bring out the inchoate tensions within the group."

"Just so," Suzie said. "The question of desire: What do these characters want? What obstacles block their way? What conflicts might emerge within and between these imaginary people? How do we raise the stakes?"

"Sure," Jim said. "If you're into the psychologized liberal self. I was thinking more the deterritorialization and reterritorialization of the assemblage."

The secretary of defense would neither confirm nor deny allegations of American drone strikes in Venezuela.

"Gotcha," Suzie said, drinking the last of her coffee. "The assemblage."

Jim's cheek twitched. "Yes."

"Well, then," Suzie said. "Let's fucking assemble."

"You gonna wear those sunglasses all day?" Jim asked.

"Are you?"

"Let's go," he said, standing up.

On their way out, Remy observed that the Muzak was Neil Young's "Walk On," which he said seemed like a good omen.

They drove and drove and drove, listening to the radio, switching between Contemporary Christian Beats and NPR, the green Valiant rolling beneath thick skies and transient cloudbursts, past green hills and trees reflected in mirrors and glass, more trees, cornfields, soybean fields, gas stations, driverless semis, college kids in old manual-steering beaters, now and then somebody asleep behind the wheel as the car drove. Waves of water fell from the sky then cleared, flushing the world gold black gray and blue.

"I wish there were more Amish," Jim said. "Or at least Mennonites."

Remy caught the light.

"How about lunch in Somerset?" Jim said. "I wanna stop in Somerset."

"What's in Somerset?" Suzie asked.

"Somerset is known for its sizeable wind farm," Remy replied from the back. "It was also one of the towns involved in the Whiskey Rebellion."

"The what?" Suzie said.

"The Whiskey Rebellion. In 1791, George Washington's government imposed the nation's first federal tax, on distilled spirits, as part of Alexander Hamilton's plan to pay off debts incurred fighting the Revolutionary War. Whiskey distillers in the frontier regions—specifically and especially western Pennsylvania—resisted, first because they considered it taxation without representation, second because whiskey was, on the frontier, a form of currency. By 1794, the resistance had erupted into armed insurrection, centered around Monongehala, south of Pittsburgh. The preacher Harmon Husband, one of the rebellion's leaders, was from Somerset."

"Well?" Suzie said. "What happened?"

"The federal government raised a thirteen-thousand-man militia and marched on western Pennsylvania. The insurrection collapsed without a fight, and some two dozen leaders were indicted on charges of high treason. I don't quite recall what happened then. I believe a few were hanged. Also near Somerset—actually closer to Shanksville—is the Flight Ninety-Three National Memorial."

"Do you just memorize Wikipedia?" she asked.

"I'm a robot," Remy said.

"I thought you preferred 'digital person,'" she said, not sure if he was joking.

"I do research. I have a list of interesting sights along likely routes, and I review each day's route the night before. I make notes. I remember things. Also I know a guy who wrote a book about it. The Whiskey Rebellion. He went to Oberlin."

"You know they fucking shot that plane down, right?" Jim said.

"Wait, what?" Suzie said.

"Flight 93. Shot down by American F-16 Falcons. On the vice president's orders."

"You believe that? Like jet fuel can't melt steel beams?"

"I don't know about that, but listen. The black box was faked. The call was faked. Cell phones don't operate over thirty thousand feet. Try it next time you fly."

"Cell phones?"

"Yeah, try it. All that 'Let's roll,' it's fucking bullshit."

"So you want to visit the memorial?"

"No, no, fuck all that. It's a smear in a field. The Whiskey Rebellion is interesting, in juxtaposition—I mean, they're both stories about the federal government killing Americans—but the resonances . . ." Jim's words trailed off.

Suzie lit a Parliament and cracked the window.

"Gettysburg, Whiskey Rebellion, Flight Ninety-Three," Jim muttered. "George, George, Abraham and Isaac, God will provide the ram."

"What are you talking about?"

"The mere proximity of events sets them ringing. History accretes, blood soaks into the earth, the air grows thick with ghosts. Too many bodies. But the ramdom . . . Ha. God will provide the deep surface."

"You okay?" Suzie asked.

"Look, what's the connection? Decades separate each event, more than a century between Gettysburg and Flight Ninety-Three, but they infect the geography of the mind. They resonate off each other. They warp our map of the world, like gravity warps space-time, drawing each discrete event into every other, one by one, each into each in totality. One by one, the events collide together until they initiate the singularity, everything collapsing in a great black involution, the holy rectum of the cosmos, and we shall be reborn in blood and fire . . . Or not. Or it's just land, rock, and water, and my brain insists it coheres in a rational pattern. What does one thing have to do with another? How does the left hand connect to the right? One day and the next, nothing, nothing, or everything all together, and the strongest pull is the story, cause and effect, here and there, but it's also the most delusional, because there is no story . . . And . . . But . . . Going back again, making it make sense is the only way it makes sense. That's the fucking rub, Suzie Q. Why are these monkey brains so primitive and superstitious? And how can it be that that selfsame savage thought is the only chance we ever get at enlightenment? Riddle me that."

Eye roll. "I dunno, Gene. Sounds pretty deep."

Jim snorted. Suzie smoked. Remy watched the fields and trees and trucks.

Lunch at Mel's. According to the Somerset *Daily American*, read between them at the table, a local veteran was going to be honored and a Latrobe man had been injured in a fall. Temperatures were higher than historical averages for the twenty-eighth month in a row. After the meal Suzie got up and went to the bathroom.

Jim looked in his wallet. "You two fuck?"

Remy blinked owlishly. "What's that?"

"You. Two. Fuck."

"No. Not . . ." Remy took a sip of coffee. "No, Jim. We didn't."

"I mean, I'd hit that shit," Jim said, taking off his mirror-shades. "For real. Bet she sucks cock like a champ."

"Wouldn't know, Jim. We smoked and talked. These comments—"

"Oh, I bet you talked. Myea myea myea." Jim jammed his middle finger in Remy's face. "You fingerblast her, huh? Get up all in that shit?" Remy leaned back, not answering, not taking his eyes off Jim. "She's pretty old, I guess, for you," Jim went on. "Couple miles of rough road, know what I mean? Pussy's probably chewed up like coleslaw."

"Jim, that's inappropriate."

"Hit it or quit it, that's what I say. Go big or go home. You know?"

People were looking now. "Jim—"

"Listen, Superfly, we're making a movie. This ain't no *Love Boat*. Slam that trim if you want, but if you do, I need close-ups. Got me?"

Something cold kindled in Remy's blue eyes. "Jim, we have worked together for a long time, and you need—"

"I need?" Jim stood up. "I need? How 'bout you need. Who's the big dog? Huh?"

Suzie came out of the bathroom and started walking toward them. "Jim—" Remy said.

Jim reached for his fly. "I will piss in your fucking face right now."

"Fine," Remy said. "You're the big dog. Just sit down."

Suzie came up to the table. "What the fuck, you two? Why's everybody staring?"

"Mythology," Jim said to Remy. Then he put his sunglasses back on. "Let's get outta here." He went to pay the check.

Suzie shot Remy a questioning look, but he shook his head and turned away.

They passed Wheeling at around three-thirty, and just the other side of town traffic slowed to a crawl. While they inched ahead, waiting to see the obstruction, they did Suzie's pages.

"Behold: muscles taut under fame's blazing corona, women throwing themselves at my feet, masses of grown men chanting my name till their throats grow hoarse and can chant no more, sleeping children dreaming of my face. I was a hero! A champion! A Trojan!"

He watched her watching him as he chanted under the green sodium glow, her ironic glasses, her smooth, straight hair. She slouched a little, and he'd begun to cherish the way the curve of her shoulder fell against the curves of her breasts, breasts he found himself wanting to palpate. It wasn't in the plan, exactly, but it wasn't not in the plan either, and whatever had passed between her and Remy was equally up for grabs. She had a way with her sharp green eyes of both daring and laughing at once, as if part of the challenge was taking the idea of daring itself seriously, which only made the dare more serious.

He spread his arms and went on shouting: "America! The pulsing flesh of your dreams, the sacred orange skin of the world in my hand like a spear, a sword, an intercontinental ballistic missile. I am a man among men, immortal youth, and this my monument: To America! To High School! To Hoosiers!"

Stay focused on the burn along the black line into

nothing, wheels on fire, a Bible and a gun. Fuck her if you want, Jim, but remember she's only a servant of the dust god, like you no more than a piece of the puzzle and the death dream we're dreaming together.

"You like my monologue?" he asked.

"Is that what that was?"

"You know," he said, "you'd be kinda hot if it weren't for your fucked-up face."

She nodded. "High praise coming from a cross-eyed fink too dumb to take off his sunglasses at night."

"The hell's a fink? That even a word?"

"Read a book."

"I would, but being cross-eyed makes it hard. Really: what'd you think?"

"I think you showed good judgment outsourcing the writing."

"Yeah?"

"Yeah."

"Why don't *you* say something, then?"

"I'm a writer, Gene. That means I write shit down and think about it. I edit out some noise, put in other noise. I don't do improv."

"Yeah, well, there was plenty of noise in your pages today."

"No problem, boss man. You want something different?"

"I want you to tell me what you think."

The buzzing lamps, the crickets' sawing chirp, the velvet embrace of the hot, wet air. She scuffed her Cons on the parking-lot blacktop. "I think you're full of shit, Gene. Which, in and of itself, is not bad or even unusual. Art's mostly bullshit, but the best stuff, right, the crème de la bullshit, is so highly refined and audacious and dense that nobody cares whether it's bullshit or not. The good stuff is pretense transcending its artifice to become a new fact in the world: nature created by human hands. Now I've seen your footage, I grok your aesthetics, and it's clear that you can make bullshit as serene and haunting as anything. But does it transcend? That I don't know. The problem, I think, is that your images are weighed down by all these dumb ideas. The problem is that your pseudo-philosophical culture-theory Deleuzian bullshit sounds, looks, and smells like bullshit. I don't even think *you* believe it. You're not an intellectual, and I'm not convinced that you really think *intellectually* about basketball or Gettysburg or anything. I think you're mostly a dick with a camera."

He smiled a sad, complicated smile, feeling wounded and turned on. He walked over to the tripod by the Valiant where the camera was running and stood there for long minutes staring at the Fieldhouse. Suzie smoked a Parliament. The moon, a white parenthesis, left the sky an open empty censored sentence over six acres of parking lot bounded down one edge by a wide, nondescript brick building and its monumental sign bearing the school's sigil, a strangely abstract Greek helmet, the name of the building, and the exhortation GO TROJANS! MAKE AMERICA GREAT AGAIN!

Jim disconnected the camera from its mount. He put the tripod in the car and pointed the camera at the Fieldhouse. "You know, out of the ten largest high-school gyms in America, nine of them are in Indiana. What does that say to you?"

"Hoosiers like basketball?"

"You have some condition that makes you state the obvious?" he snapped.

"I think of it as a gift," she said. "Look, I don't know what you want, Gene. What should I say? This means something? It's a thin substitute for killing Indians or Japs or Muslims? You want me to say something about the poor, overcivilized American sap who doesn't have any way to act out his primal urges except through the voyeurism of the sports field, where he watches boy whores destroy themselves in racialized gladiatorial psychodrama, and it's money and advertising and patriotism and spectacle and what are you supposed to do, you schlep, you sad motherfucker? Is that any less fucking obvious? We all know what's going on, Gene. Everybody already knows the score." She flicked her butt off into the parking lot. "Is that sort of what you had in mind?"

"Yeah. Do that some more," he said.

"Fuck, man. I think there's something seriously wrong with you."

He turned the camera toward her. "I know there's something wrong with me. But that's not the question. I also know there's something wrong with America. But that's not the question, either." He turned the camera back toward the Fieldhouse. "The question that interests me, Suzie, is are they the same thing."

"Seriously?" she asked.

"Listen. The Nenets shamans of the Taymyr Peninsula fight disease by doing battle with the spirit of the disease, inside their soul. Some plague comes to your village and you, the village *tadibya*, deliberately infect yourself so you can struggle with the demon and learn its ways. Learn how to defeat it. You take on the disease to find the cure."

"And you think you're a shaman?"

"It's a *metaphor*. Fuck Christ. You of all people should not have to be so goddamn literal. They must teach metaphor in your fancy-ass workshops, right? At the New School? It's like this: There's something wrong with me, and I'm not sure what it is. There's something wrong with America, and I'm not sure what that is. There's something happening, a new warp forming out of the old pattern. You've seen it, it's the dream ballet that haunts your sleep, reality kaleidoscoping around us. Where are we going? In what form will the new pattern crystallize? Is it a death assemblage? Or is it a door through to something else? I don't know. All I can see is the rush to the void, the blood chaos vortexing into the bottleneck. But maybe if I get out in front . . . scout ahead . . . maybe I can find a way through."

He hadn't meant to say so much. It was a risk putting things into words, sharing them with other people. Now he waited, wary, while she processed. He watched her follow him up to a point, then balk at the precipice. Most did.

"Why do you even care about America?" she said, diverting. "It's not even real. It's just a name for a government, a label for a surveillance state, a long con. America's bullshit."

"Just like art," he said. "So grandiose and stirring nobody cares it's bullshit. We must have meaning. We—*WE*—must exist, held together by collective stress and fantasy. Apple pie. Tea Party. The Wild West. John Wayne. Barack Obama.

Anyone can grow up to be president. Private property. The truths we hold to be self-evident."

"That all white, Christian, property-owning men are created equal," she said.

"America. The world. Whatever. The point is the vision. We're not even there yet. This is just act one."

She relaxed a little, seeing him—really seeing him—for perhaps the first time. "So what's your vision, Gene?"

He remembered the wreck they'd passed earlier, the smashed Toyota and the toppled truck, human-shaped shapes covered in red-smeared white, the blinking, flashing red and blue lights so festive. The smell of burning flesh and electrical wire coming in the window as they rolled slowly past, melting insulation, melting plastic, charred hair. Hot wind rising from the highway.

Rise of the machines, he'd said at the time, half joking. But what he'd been thinking inside was *freedom*.

"When I close my eyes," he said, "I see a red desert, black lines, highway to the horizon. I see a point, lines, and space. Pure acceleration. Fire on the mountain. That's where we start over."

"So what are we doing in Indiana?" Suzie asked.

"Killing time."

"Okay, well, I think I'm about done killing time for the night."

He turned off the camera. "I've got a bottle of Maker's in my room. Why don't you come up and we can do your pages together?"

She made a face, like disappointment or maybe contempt, he couldn't quite parse it. Her reaction cheered him, though, because it meant she'd say yes, eventually. Such things were scripted.

"I can do the pages myself, thanks. That's what you pay me for, boss man." She started for the Valiant.

"I know you can," he said, watching her ass sway in her black jeans. "But maybe I can offer some suggestions. The pages today felt off."

She turned on him. "This isn't a tango, Gene. I write my words. Not some hive-mind consensus, not the world—me. I pick. My process. Unlike you, I recognize a difference between my mind and reality, and while I draw from reality to do my making, what I turn out is mine, my own thing. It's not all the same. You're paying for it, so if you have feedback, tell me what you want and I'll try to write it like that. But as for hands-on, that wasn't in our contract."

He let it go until they got back to the hotel, when he switched off the growling V8 and looked thoughtfully at the steering wheel, putting on his best poised internal struggle. He held it, the two of them sitting in the dark while the engine's rumble faded into the slow tick of the cooling block.

"Look," he said, "I was asking you up. I know it's not appropriate. I just . . . it's been difficult since Carol left . . . I've been . . . it's been really hard to . . . feel things . . . But you . . ." He looked over at her, then up at the windshield, inhaling, blinking as if holding back tears. "You make me feel things."

"Oh for fuck's sake," Suzie said, opening the door and half sliding out before turning back to look at him. This time he was sure it was contempt. "If this is some shit between you and Remy, duke it out on your time. I'm not a fucking football."

"I—" Jim began.

Suzie cut him off: "If, by some chance," she went on, "you just genuinely, truly, madly, deeply want to get into my pants, you're gonna have to do better than *feelings*. It's fucking sad. S–A–D *sad*. But you know what, sad man who's sad, I'll give you some tech support. A little lesson in scoring with grown-ass women. You got to get over this 'I can help you with your homework' fucking *bullshit*. Just ask me, like an adult, if I'd like to come up and fuck. Try saying, 'Suzie, I think you're very attractive, and I'd like to have sex with you. Would you like to come up to my room and fuck?'"

His cheeks flushed and his pants felt tight. She was even more appealing than before, somehow, and the blood pounding in his ears seemed the only sound he'd ever heard. "Suzie," he said, his throat thick, giving her his best Ryan Gosling, "I think you're very attractive. Would you like to come up and fuck?"

"No," she said. "Not with you. Not ever." Then the door slammed and she was gone.

The roaring in his ears crashed like a roof caving in, and he got out and shouted her name across the lot as she disappeared inside the hotel. "Fuck," he screamed, slamming his fist into the Valiant's green fender, then "Fuck" again when the pain pierced his red-clouded mind like a white wire. He locked the Valiant and walked around the parking lot, once, twice, and again, then went up to his room and took a shower, poured himself some whiskey, and drank and watched TV until he fell asleep, muttering every now and again fuck fucking frigid fucking cunt fuck fuck.

Bleach sun shuddering humid over endless yellow-sprouting cornfields, low green rows of soy, off-white box architecture, strip malls and highways, highways and parking lots, parking lots brilliant with the shine of two hundred sixty million gas-powered combustion-engine personal-transit devices, five billion three hundred million metric tons of carbon dioxide rising up over billboards reading PORN DESTROYS LOVE and JESUS IS COMING and IN THE BEGINNING GOD CREATED . . .

They rolled west and southwest, leaving behind the last frontiers, riding the jade Valiant across the scarred back of America, the wide flat plane broken by crossed lines of fiber-optic cable, natural gas, oil, and concrete, the seemingly endless and endlessly fertile acreage of Monsanto and Cargill and Dow, Beck's Hybrids and Tyson and JBS United, the holy sweep of waving wheat and heavy-headed barley, red sorghum and golden canola, pig factories and chicken factories and cattle factories, land once wide with white oak savannas, fed by flooding rivers, ruled by warrior nomads who lived without knowing the fear of death, land once home to massed flocks and herds of black-eyed beasts so innumerable they darkened the skies and shook the earth with their passing, buffalo and passenger pigeon, antelope, heron, elk, and puma, land now roamed by driverless semis

and robot tractors, all automated slaughterhouses, automated factories, automated farms, this land they drove
down into, entering the heart of the thing, a heart bounded
in concrete and prefab, tract homes surrounded by waste
lots.

"Democracy!" Suzie read. "Near at hand to you a throat
is now inflating itself and joyfully singing! *Ma femme!* For
the brood beyond us and of us, for those who belong here
and those to come, I exultant to be ready for them will now
shake out carols stronger and haughtier than have ever yet
been heard upon the earth!"

Things at breakfast had been strained, conversation awk-
ward. Indianapolis, Monrovia, Cloverdale.

The water from the tap hard and bitter. The skies hazy
gray. The smell of chickenshit and pigshit stinks in from
miles off, making them wonder for long minutes if something's dead in the vents before finally seeing the meat
factory in the distance, its simmering lake of fecal slop blazing in the sun's rays.

Highway patrol, weigh stations, Shell, Arco, Conoco.
Terre Haute, Casey, Greenup, Teutopolis, Effingham.

"I will make the songs of passion to give them their way,"
Suzie read, "and your songs outlawed offenders, for I scan
you with kindred eyes, and carry you with me the same as
any."

Altamont, Vandalia, Greenville, Granite City. Amoco,
ExxonMobil, BP.

The first few days they ran high on the feeling of novelty,
excited by the project and the promise of it, the sensory
shock of going from New York schiz to hours sitting

cramped in rolling steel. They read Suzie's pages, they read a Gideon Bible, they read a copy of *Leaves of Grass* Suzie had brought along to raise the intellectual tenor of the project. They talked about their favorite sushi restaurants, movies they'd seen recently, the last show they binge-watched, Twitter and Snapchat and fake news, how fucked up America was and could you believe it. They argued about whether or not it mattered to vote in presidential elections, discussed people they knew who knew somebody who'd served in Afghanistan or Iraq or Syria or Korea or Mexico, reminisced about places they'd traveled. Remy gave mini-lectures, prepared from notes and Wikipedia, on Missouri's statehood, demographic changes across the Great Plains during World War II, the history of the John Birch Society, and the rise of the Koch brothers. Suzie tried to explain Melville's *The Confidence-Man* to Jim, but gave up and promised to buy him a copy next time they came to a Barnes & Noble and read it to him in the car. Despite whatever interpersonal and romantic tensions might have given the hours a certain piquant tang, it still had all seemed like fun, like a road trip, until they turned south and the air began to thicken around them. The sun's heat turned sour, perverse, and the car became a baking box.

"What are those, cicadas?" Remy asked. "It's like the soundtrack to *Psycho*."

East St. Louis, Pacific, Union. Lunch at Hagie's 19 after a fierce debate over whether Subway was real food or not.

Soon the car became another cell, too much the same four interior surfaces, same burning metal and leather, same cube rolling over monotonous gray-black roads through

monotonous gray-green highway emptiness, same songs on
the radio, same assumptions and expectations, same plot,
same stops, same beginning, same end, same Suzie and
Remy and Jim steeping in their body odor. 76, Unocal,
Grandee's Big Jim's Truck Stop, St. Clair, Sullivan, Bourbon,
Cuba, St. James, Rolla, Newburg, Waynesville, Lebanon,
Phillipsburg, Conway, Marshfield, Springfield.

"I will make the true poem of riches," Suzie read, "to
earn for the body and the mind whatever adheres and goes
forward and is not dropt by death; I will effuse egotism and
show it underlying all, and I will be the bard of personality,
and I will show male and female that either is the equal of
the other, and sexual organs and acts! Do you concentrate
in me, for I am determined to tell you with courageous
clear voices to prove you illustrious, and I will show that
there is no imperfection in the present, and can be none in
the future, and I will show that whatever happens to anybody it may be turned to beautiful results, and I will show
that nothing can happen more beautiful than death."

Republic, Mount Vernon, Sarcoxie, Joplin, Neosho, Fort
Crowder, Goodman, Anderson, Pineville, Bella Vista, Ben-
tonville, Lowell, Flying J, Petro, Love's, Pilot.

Suzie smoked and watched for roadkill. Now with all of
them implicated, she had to be on all the time, the energy
charged and fragile and feral, and she couldn't let her weak
side show to either one at any point for fear they'd push
their advantage to extremes. In the night, alone in her room,
she let herself remember that she liked them both, more or
less, and that even still Jim's damaged rich-boy drama held
a darkly glimmering appeal, whereas Remy on the other

hand was comforting in an abstract way, like a Mies van der Rohe chair. Thinking through the narrative possibilities, the options narrowed to one or two sustainable outcomes: either she hooked up with Jim, or she hooked up with no one and they kept their precarious balance as professionals. A sustained coupling with Remy would drive Jim out of his head, leave her disappointed and restless, and endanger the trip. Some kind of easy trio would be the utopian option, though she doubted Jim went for that kind of thing. No, the sexual politics of the situation, given their gender identities and bodies, presented only two choices, and those choices, knowing herself, seemed to narrow to one. Yet she refused to accept the inevitability of her and Jim fucking, first because she believed she was free to decide what she wanted—she wasn't some fucking algorithm—and second because he was a jerk. So for the time being it was walk the line, but you know what, she thought, fuck that. I do what I want.

Springdale, Chicken Capital of the World! Tyson Foods, Inc. They have another fight that night, this time over who's supposed to clean the trash out of the car, then split for their rooms, tensions high. Suzie goes to Remy's room and they get high and watch a *Westworld* rerun, then she goes to bed alone. At breakfast there's an argument about whether or not they should go deeper into Arkansas, finally settled two to one against, Remy and Suzie aligning to block Jim. Jim sees what's happening and it infuriates him, but he's a patient man. Anyway, this movie is scripted. They hit 412 west for OKC.

Mostly she missed her cat, her routine, and although she

hated her work and the stupid constant crises, she found she missed that, too, just the comfort of the routine. Was she turning into the kind of person who'd rather stay home? The one who lets things go? And if so, is it just a function of age, or some slippage in her character? She wasn't really sure anymore who she was exactly: something more or less than a big weird bug stuck on the inside of a southbound windshield. Also, after the jolt of novelty wore off, the long silence and flat land freed her mind to reflect on the past in a way not often available in the hunter-predator crowd-splicing attention economy of the digital urban day. This reflection was something she didn't particularly welcome; it was painful and sad and confusing to think back on her family, her childhood, her life on the plains and elsewhere, the choices she'd made. One time she almost burst into tears because she remembered a birthday present someone gave her childhood best friend when they were both little, she must have been seven, a sparkly charm necklace reading PRINCESS. Suzie stole the necklace one night when she slept over, then buried it in a hole in her yard, motivated by envy perhaps or just malice, and the mingled rush of pleasure, fear, and guilt that hit her when she saw her friend crying over the lost charm made her flesh tingle even today. What an awful thing, she thought, and how am I any better now? When was the last time I saw—what was her name—Christie? Krista? Crystal? Would I apologize if I saw her today, or keep it to myself? Or forget again what happened?

Siloam Springs, Chouteau, Inola, Texaco, Citgo, Philips 66.

"I will not make poems with reference to parts," she

chanted, "but I will make poems, songs, thoughts, with reference to ensemble, and I will not sing with reference to a day, but with reference to all days, and I will not make a poem nor the least part of a poem but has reference to the soul, because having looked at the objects of the universe, I find there is no one nor any particle of one but has reference to the soul."

Tulsa, Sapulpa, Bristow, Stroud, Davenport, Sinclair, Sunoco, Chevron.

Jim, on the other hand, despite his irritation, was secretly pleased, for although the driving was getting pretty goddamned boring, they were over the transition and beginning to settle into the thing itself, which was developing a pleasant edge. All this was almost exactly what he'd had in mind, and he looked forward to more fights and was happy because the animal is never more alive than when it's fighting. He wanted them together but estranged, and it was all shaping up quite nicely. He thought ahead to the desert, the wind and sand and burn, and thought of his Colt buried deep in his rolling suitcase, its weight, the smell of slick oil, the firm feel of the heavy rounds, the barrel's hard thrust. He imagined Suzie howling in the juniper, half mad, her voice worn to its last ragged human strains—and he couldn't help but smile, glad for the challenge and thrilled at the prospect of it, the autonomy of art. He wondered if she would cry. Oh, she was tough, no question. But everyone had their breaking point. Then he'd pick up the pieces and she'd look at him so gratefully, so tenderly, it would change everything.

Travel Centers of America, Valero, Chandler, Wellston.

Remy filmed her mounting the steps to the western gate, the afternoon sun flashing off the bronze wall and the numbers over the entry. She walked with grace and slowly, trailing white, veiled in white, carrying a white bouquet.

"That's good," Jim said. "Just like that."

She passed through the doorway, framed between the bronze and the emptiness of the cotton-streaked Oklahoma blue, 9:03 above her like the name of a god.

"Stay on the door, now, don't focus on the number, don't focus on the inscription. Just let it zoom out very, very slowly until we get the street and the cars and everything."

Remy held the camera level on its tripod, letting it run, then began to do what Jim asked, slowly opening out to the rest of the world. As the view pulled farther and farther back, the monument seemed dwarfed—not by the insignificant Oklahoma City high-rises, hotels, and government buildings, but by the immensity of heaven itself.

"Great . . . great . . . great . . . ," Jim said. "Cut."

They folded up the tripod then hustled across Harvey Avenue and through the gate, where they found Suzie leaning in the shade, fanning herself with a brochure.

"This dress is a fucking oven," she said, throwing back her veil.

"Heat wave," Remy said. "Wet bulb's supposed to get up over a hundred today."

"Awesome. Nothing near as sexy as a wedding dress with pit stains. I'm gonna smell like a trucker by the time we're done, if I don't get heat stroke first."

"I have to admit, I'm somewhat disappointed by how empty it is here," Jim said, looking out over the long, shallow memorial pool hazing in the heat, a skin of water over slabs of black granite edged by white and gray stones, which separated the eastern and western Gates of Time. To the north of the pool a few scattered trees—the Rescuers' Orchard and the Survivor Tree—framed the way up a small rise to the blocky eyesore Journal Record Building. The south side opened to a field of empty chairs, glass and bronze, surrounded by evergreen pines.

"It's eerie," said Remy. "You're from Oklahoma, Suzie. Have you been here before?"

"No, but I remember it happening. We'd just come back from Japan and I had to start junior high in the middle of the year. The bombing seemed like part of the general fuckedupness of my life at the time, like *of course* there'd be a terrorist attack."

"I didn't know you lived in Japan," Remy said.

"I tend to block it out myself."

"The brochure says the Journal Record Building houses the National Memorial Institute for the Prevention of Terrorism," said Jim. "After we're done here, I want to film that."

"Either of you gentlemen have any water?" Suzie asked.

"I'll go get some while you two shoot the next sequence," Jim said.

First he had to set up the shot. He wanted Remy right next to the gate, in the shade, and for Suzie to walk though again, ever so slowly, and for Remy to keep the camera tight on her face. Then he wanted her to drift from the gate to the edge of the pool, the camera keeping the same focus, letting her shift against the ground. There she'd take a few steps and stop, look around, not quite startled but more like she remembered something important, like she left the oven on. Then she'd take a few steps away from the pool and sort of sag, withering slightly, like she remembered the house already burned down and the oven didn't matter anymore. He wanted her to sort of waver there, standing but sinking, almost falling, almost floating, almost dropping the bouquet but not quite, then after a minute step lightly back to the pool. Then she'd walk to the east corner and delicately crumple into a fetal position.

"As you go down," he said, "drop the bouquet and clutch your hands to your stomach. Go slow. Hold the shot. Everything is about slowness. If you can shake, like racked with sobs, that'd be perfect. Make the fall last as long as you can. If anyone comes up to help or bother you or whatever, ignore them. Remy will take care of it. The whole take, from the gate to the end of the fall, should take forty minutes, so do everything real, real slow."

"You definitely better get me some water, then. And some Chiclets."

"Chiclets?"

"You got breath rike Gojira. Maybe the pork enchilada you had for lunch, I don't know, but I can hardly hear you right now, Gene-san, 'cuz you reeky rike shitbomb."

"Fine," he said. "Just go really, really slow. If you go too fast, we'll have to do the whole thing over."

"What about interference?" Remy asked.

"Let it bounce," he said. "I'll be back in a minute and then I can handle any hard stuff. Let's set up."

So they set up and Suzie went back out the gate and Jim watched Remy film her walk slow, ever so slow, yet graceful and easy, yes, spectral. When he was satisfied with her speed and confident the shot would take the right amount of time, he went around the gate and into the street, past a statue of Jesus weeping, searching for some kind of corner store.

Jim looked up and down the street, trying to rely on his city sense to guide him toward the nearest store, a sense that in New York could hardly fail to uncover a bodega anywhere but in the most denuded wastes. Here, though, he had little luck, and had to walk five blocks before finding a Panera stuck awkwardly on an otherwise empty street. He bought several bottles of water and three iced teas, and by the time he got back to the memorial Suzie was just collapsing, ever so slowly, at the corner of the pool. It looked just like he wanted, maybe even better. He watched, entranced by seeing his imagination come to life, as she folded in on herself and then shook, painful and tender, like a virgin being stabbed by the finest ancient bone blade. Remy held it for a full ten minutes and, although some of the pedestrians walking through the memorial gawked, none of them blocked the shot. Perfect. When Remy stopped the camera, Jim clapped. "Great," he shouted, and Suzie sat up smiling, giving him a thumbs-up. Jim headed around the pool while Remy dismounted the camera.

"Good?" she asked.

"Superb. You really earned your water."

"Thanks."

"I got you an iced tea, too. You walk really well."

"Practice, man, practice." After taking a long drink of water, she stretched her legs in front of her, leaned back on one hand, and lit a cigarette. "What next?"

Jim looked over at the glass and bronze chairs. "I got some ideas," he said.

They shot into the afternoon, tracking Suzie walking among the chairs and around the Survivor Tree. As the day wore on, she began to wonder what Jim thought he was getting at with all this footage. None of it quite cohered. The bombing remained for her wedged into a particular moment in her life, a media-historical blister erupting out of her own junior-high anomie, or so it felt, mixed into the grim spring of the O. J. Simpson trial and war in Bosnia, a little after Kurt Cobain blew his brains out and a little before whatever the rest of the nineties were, dial-up, MySpace, Monica Lewinsky. Or was MySpace later? She remembered vaguely what the story had been, some militia nut and his buddies drove a truck full of homemade explosives down from Michigan, something like that. And wasn't he a vet? Gulf War? Panama? She wished she had her phone so she could look it up. From the plaque, she knew one hundred sixty-eight people had died, nineteen of them children. According to the informational brochure, "three unborn children died along with their mothers." Their names were listed on their mothers' chairs. She remembered Lieutenant Colonel Oliver North testifying in the Iran-Contra hearings on TV, visiting Genbaku Dome at Hiroshima with her dad when they were stationed in Japan, antiaircraft tracers rising up out of Baghdad on CNN when the US started bombing Iraq the first time, the artist's sketch of the Unabomber in a hoodie and mirrorshades, Branch Davidians at Waco, the shoot-out at Ruby Ridge, and a YouTube video explaining 9/11 was an inside job. Now Nazis ran the country. What the fuck happened?

It's terrifying to realize the depth of your ignorance, the incoherent ignorance of your own past, the confused ignorance of your present, and to see that your life is a groping, half-blind stumble through foggy, unknown lands marked out here and there by lurid screenshots jacked into your skull by mass-media conglomerates, memes on repeat, empty concepts repeated until they become true, while your poor Paleolithic brain works overtime to connect the dots, keep the plot together, connect yesterday to tomorrow in a straight line that goes somewhere hopeful.

When they finished shooting, she asked him, "Who am I supposed to be all dressed up like this?"

"Oh, I don't know. I hadn't thought about it. The image came to me when I read about the chairs and the pool. It's ghostly, so maybe you're a ghost? The ghost of Oklahoma, maybe? The ghost of Tom Joad? Does it matter?"

"Jeez, and I was counting on you having some cockeyed gibberish ready with which to clothe this exercise in a fug of intellectual pretension."

"Nobody's perfect," Jim said. "Let's try the museum."

At the entrance was a sign reading NO PHOTOGRAPHY. NO PETS. NO MUSLIMS., so Remy ran back to the car to get what they called the ninja cam, an American flag lapel pin with a tiny spy camera. They toured the museum, read about the events of April 19, 1995, looked at the stopped clock and bits of rubble, listened to an audio recording of the explosion, watched videos at interactive computer stations explaining what survivors and others had experienced in the first hours after the attack, followed the steps of the investigation, paid their respects at the Gallery of Honor, read about the funerals and mourning that had followed, and finished in a room labeled HOPE, decorated with golden origami cranes. In the gift shop Suzie bought a T-shirt reading I ♥ OKLAHOMA.

Then they took a brief tour of the Memorial Institute for the Prevention of Terrorism, which turned out to be a reading room adjacent to some offices. Jim asked the curly-haired, matronly receptionist if he could see the institute at work, and she told him, "Honey, you done seen it. Mostly what we do is information clearinghouse, so we collect on terrorism prevention and distribute online. Here, take a brochure. We got ones on ISIS, Russian cyberterrorism, MS-13, ecoterrorists, and Black Lives Matter—maybe you've seen our website, MIPT dot org? That's where we do our real work. You can graph incidents there and connect with vigilance-training programs all over the country. Here's a brochure on MIPT, this one's on the border wall, and here's one that tells what you can do to fight global jihad."

Jim took the brochures and thanked her. They shot some more late-afternoon footage around the pool, then grabbed sandwiches at Panera and hit the road, rolling southwest into the blasted red of the setting sun, silent for miles. They did Suzie's pages. Colossal thunderheads rose into the sky, veined by sheet lightning, dumping rain across distant flats, then dissipated into the west.

Somewhere out in the plains they were overtaken by a long line of tan five-tons, Humvees, and armored personnel carriers full of faceless men in Wiley X shades and digital camo, M4 carbines jutting from windows, some trucks mounted with machine guns manned by dark-goggled grunts in armor, a sudden unfolding of combat steel into humdrum traffic.

"Get that, quick," Jim said to Remy, who turned and filmed the convoy until a machine gunner spotted him. The gunner pointed at Remy and shook his head, then drew a line across his throat. Remy lowered the camera. Truck after truck rumbled by, then they were gone.

His hand on the doorknob. The yellow lamplight falling from the end table over the couch across the floor. The cot still folded in the corner. His cheek twitches in the half-light. He slides the key card in the pocket of his khakis. His hand on the doorknob. Her hoodie on the back of the couch. His cheek twitches in the half-light.

Her voice in the next room.

The cot still folded in the corner. The moon three-quarters full through the window, his gut and rib cage. Jim stands listening for another gasp in the other room, his stomach tightening. The carpet is soft and thick, dark brown with a pattern of tiny white squares. He sees his torso reflected in the screen, sees himself caught—or waiting to catch. His hand heavy with the Colt.

He hears a quiet grunt. His cheek twitches in the half-light. The fireplace, the kitchenette, the cot still folded in the corner.

The moon in the window.

Rolling down the road toward Quartz Mountain Lodge, fattening moon plump in the wide, star-spattered sky, "Don't Be Cruel" playing on the radio. Remy's face reflecting light from the camera's viewscreen in the back, the viewscreen showing featureless black backs of heads, headlights on the road, the dotted yellow line dividing the darkness ahead. Suzie turns to face Jim in silhouette, talking, her glasses in silhouette, lips talking. The dashboard lights submarine green, an attack chopper.

Eyes gleam stray light.

The car's hum a womb. The car itself a womb, metal and hum. The world outside wraps like black tape or reels of film. The Valiant rolls, and in the distance they can see the resort's lights shining like the promised land, reflected in the black lake below, moon shining in the black lake below, now there's two of everything.

She walks away down the low hill edging the black lake, leaving Jim standing by the small tree, leaving Jim silhouetted against the fat white moon.

Suzie turns and walks down the hill.

The hill, in the dark, under the moon, over the lake. A mysterious hill, a portentous hill, a hill made for a Chickasaw brave to ride up to be painted by Remington—lean torso, tragic mien. Suzie shakes her head and turns away and walks down the hill.

Wind spills from the innumerable stars and whispers along the lake and Suzie walks down.

Jim turns to her. Jim turns and reaches, pulling her toward him. Suzie breaks away and says something, crosses her arms across her chest. He says something back and she shakes her head. She shakes her head and turns and walks down the hill, leaving Jim standing by the small tree, silhouetted against the fat white three-quarters moon.

In the lobby a drunk in a shiny gray suit sits leaning, elbows on knees. A woman with spangly earrings and blonde hair and brown roots stands off to the side, fists on her hips, staring beyond the door into the dark.

Across the lobby through the door to the dining room they can see a party, hear the tinkle of glasses and chatter. The clerk tells them they're very lucky, very lucky indeed—there's a wedding on, but they have one cabin left, a two-bedroom suite, and they can bring up a cot.

All the way from New York, huh?

A woman stumbles out of the dining room laughing her head off, followed by a red-faced man lunging at her.

The clerk hopes they'll have the chance to enjoy Quartz Mountain Lodge's many great features, including its eighteen-hole golf course, interpretive hiking, spelunking, Olympic pool, and volleyball courts.

They load out their gear into the cabin. Remy says he'll take the cot.

The shore of the lake damp from rain. The moon rolls gently in the black water. A coyote yips.

He glances at her walking next to him in the dark, her suspicious eyes gleaming and her ripe lips drawn in a tight line. She's wearing her I ♥ OKLAHOMA T-shirt and a thin black hoodie. He notices again how tall she is, nearly as tall as he is, and feels again the desire to put his hands on her hips and draw her close.

She walks alongside and can feel him looking, making plans. She wonders which movie this is. She wonders if she'll let it happen. Maybe tonight with the moon and his stubble and the moist thick air, maybe tonight after filming, maybe the moon and lake and stars.

He's talking and she listens and talks back.

Coyotes cry in the distance. Stars glimmer.

We're all like the moon tonight, Remy thinks, standing in the dark outside the cabin, seeing everything cold and distant. Witnessing. It's a nice night for it.

They're out there somewhere in the moonlight with the coyotes, and he knows there are two ways they could come back. And if together . . . Well, what business is it of his? It's not as if she's the last lover on earth, not as if he didn't already have enough going on back in the city, not as if he couldn't Grindr up some action in an hour if he wanted, once they returned to civilization, so what's the fuss? Why the cathexis? But there was something, wasn't there? Was it Jim? They'd never competed before, not for anything. Remy always bowed his head and let Jim run things, let Jim do whatever Jim wanted. It was Jim's money. Jim's camera. He was just the hired eye.

Why is it different now? Is it her? Is it them? The weird shit at the diner? The road? You change the environment, you change the being. Where does desire come in?

Do what you will.

Do what you do.

Hold up, step back, and *film*. Be the camera.

The moon above, promising everything. America and love and a whole new you. Narrative tension, climax, resolution.

You remember sitting at the kitchen table in your apartment back in Middletown and Nina was over and you wanted to get into her pants so bad, you'd been working her three whole weeks trying to make it, and you finally had her over and you thought Chuck was out of town for the weekend, Chuck the Superfuck, that's what homeboy called himself. But no, there he was, and as soon as he started flirt-ing with Nina, what'd you do? Did you tell him to fuck off, take Nina into your room, close the door? No. You with-drew. You felt distant and then you were distant and then you were filming him in your mind, him, her, them, you took an anthropological, aesthetic interest in their mating behaviors, and later on, after you all got high, it was his bed she slept in. Nina with the Angela Davis gap in her teeth and those really quite enormous breasts. And you beat off in your room listening to them fuck, imagining you were there, in the mix, giving and receiving, fucking, getting fucked, because after all it wasn't just Nina you wanted.

The moon making promises, he thinks, looking up at her walking down the trail from the lake, alone, smoking. He waits for her to come to him, witnessing.

The moon in the window.

Jim's hand on the bedroom doorknob. The yellow lamp-light falling from the end table across the couch and floor. The cot still folded in the corner. His cheek twitches in the half-light. His hand on the doorknob. Her hoodie on the back of the couch. His hand heavy.

Her voice behind the door, rhythmic, quietly driving. *If it's our trip, it's my trip. I understand us. I understand we. I understand collectivity. I get to drive.*

The cot still folded in the corner. The moon three-quarters full through the cabin window, through the opening between the curtains, through gut and rib cage. Jim stands listening, listening for another gasp, his stomach and crotch tighten-ing. The carpet is soft and thick, dark brown with tiny gray squares. He sees his torso reflected in the screen, the silver gleam of his cavalry Colt. His empty left hand curls in a fist over the doorknob.

He hears her grunt, twice, three times. His cheek twitches in the half-light. The fireplace, kitchenette, cot folded in the corner. The moon in the room, three-quarters full, making promises.

Horses and whispers. She walks along the split-rail fence before the horses staring, dust rising around their hooves. A man comes through the gate in the fence. He's got a face like a blob of wet dough with two eyeholes poked in and a flap of skin for a mouth. "You walk on water," he says, "and fly away. Feel it in your hands, here," he says, taking her hand in his and pushing into her forearm with his fingers, then into the crook of her elbow, "and here."

She backs into the fence. "I've got stuff to do," she says.

"Steve?" the man says, then makes a fluttering sound with his mouth flap: *Hltltltltltltlt.*

She climbs over the fence down into an alley on the Lower East Side, where a shapeless feathered skinsuit digs in cans. The buildings go all the way up, exposed brick, the sky lost somewhere in foggy, artificially distressed gray clouds. Pixels gel, freeze, and flow. She's aware of the fact that Steve is somewhere alone, crying, left to his own devices, which are few and insubstantial. She feels bad and knows she needs to feed him, but where's the kibble?

She looks under a dumpster. He likes to hide *under* things. She hopes there are some cars up ahead, so she can look *under* them, but the alley just keeps going.

Then one of the walls shudders with a boom-boom-boom.

She edges back along the other side and sees through a window that opens onto the lower city buildings burning, a jet engine burning, a mob of white-hooded Klansmen praying to the fire.

"Steve," she shouts.

There's movement and the light shifts.

"Steve," she shouts.

"Breakfast time, kids," Jim's voice through the door. "We gotta go."

She sat up and reached past Remy for her glasses. "Just a minute," multicolored blocks falling into place in her mind. The moon on the lake, the moon through the window. She could see summer sun now shining through the crack between the drapes. Clothes all over the floor.

"Well, hurry up, then," Jim shouted through the door.

"Hold your goddamned horses," she shouted back.

Remy rolled over, observing her sleepily. "Who's Steve?" he asked.

"My cat," she said. She thought about kissing him, then just patted his hip. "Boss man wants to get moving."

Remy blinked. "Yeah?"

"Yeah."

He made a face. "Whoops."

"Whoops what?"

"Whoops, I don't know." His eyes changed color at her, green to gray. "Are you . . . Do you think he's upset?"

"At what?"

"At us. That we . . ."

"That we fucked?"

"Yes. That we slept together."

"I'm pretty sure he's pissed," she said. "Is that a problem?"

"It could be," he said, getting up. Suzie watched him for a minute as he pulled on his pants, looking at the scar across his chest that had disturbed and intrigued her last night. He was slim but flabby, the kind of natural beanpole who never needed the gym, built for hallways and conference rooms. The liver-gray scar ran across his solar plexus, just below his sternum, a deep and lurid trench cut into soft ocher flesh. Maybe that was where they installed his software, she thought ungenerously as she got up to put on her underwear. She wondered how bad she smelled, whether she needed a shower, and sniffed herself. She did.

"What's it matter to him who you fuck?" she asked.

Remy frowned. "You know better than that."

"So what? We have to bend to his fucking will?"

"Suzie, Jim and I have been filming together for a long time. We have a serious professional relationship."

"Look," she cut him off. "I need a shower. You boys have whatever relationship you have, okay, and I'm not in it. You and me, Remy, we fucked last night. We had a fun time. We're consenting adults. And it's none of Jim's goddamn business. Okay? This, us—you and me, Remy—is a dyad, not a threesome."

"I wish it were so simple," Remy said. "Listen, Suzie, I think it can be managed, but we should go easy with him. Don't provoke. Don't escalate. Let him get used to things."

"It can be *managed*? Are you fucking serious?" she said, throwing clothes into her suitcase. "I need to coddle this grown-ass man? I need to account for who I have sex with to this fucking guy? My *employer*? Are you fucking kidding me?"

"I don't mean coddle him, Suzie, just give him space and respect. Let him get used to the idea, and I think he'll come around."

"I don't explain myself to anyone," she said, turning on him. "Who I fuck is none of his goddamned nevermind, and neither is it who you fuck. Maybe you should think about that."

"Suzie, please. I would only ask you to hold back a bit. Don't put him on the defensive."

"What the *fuck*, Remy? Man up. You got the equipment."

"I'm sorry?"

"Man the fuck up. You're so worried about what Jim fucking thinks, be a man for once in your life instead of his *bitch*." She shot the last word at him, stood, then turned back to her suitcase, jerking it onto the bed.

"That's not very helpful, Suzie," Remy said. "I shouldn't have to remind you that, professionally speaking, we're both Jim's employees."

"What are you, his fucking slave?" She whirled, shouting, then caught herself. Her face flushed. "I mean . . . We're not . . ."

"I know what you mean," he said, his eyes going bright and cloudy. "I guess I'll see you at breakfast."

"Remy," she said, reaching after him.

"I'll see you at breakfast." He broke away, collected the rest of his clothes, and went into the living room.

Suzie stepped out of her underwear and into the shower, gritting her teeth, and as the hot water fell over her face she hit herself in the forehead, again and again, muttering, "Fuck bitch bitch fuck bitch fuck fuck." That didn't help much, so she dug her nails into the soft flesh below her hip bones until the pain was loud enough to take the edge off the feelings.

They'd had a fine time, she and Remy, nothing special, but it had been nice to have the intimacy, however transient. A warm body meant a lot these days, whereas maybe when she was younger she didn't feel like she needed it so much. He'd been a considerate, gently aggressive lover, a tender top to her bossy bottom, and maybe it could have been the start of something. She doubted that now, and maybe it had never really been possible, given the situational algebra. In some sense, she felt like she'd known this would happen, exactly this, and she'd also known she'd never be able to depend on Remy to stand by her. She'd known all of it, from the opening sentence, and maybe this was how she'd written it.

She turned off the shower. Her hand stayed on the faucet knob, and she leaned her head against the smooth cream-colored wall. I'm done with this, she thought, done. I don't know what you think you were doing, but you've fucked it up like usual, and the best option now is to just cut loose and run. She imagined Jim's big brown eyes looking up at her from the breakfast table, like a dog you were yelling at who didn't know why.

Out in the living room, she was surprised to find Remy sitting on the couch, staring out the window at the Oklahoma plain.

"Jim went to breakfast," he said. "He told me he wanted to read the paper. Are you ready?"

"Yeah," she said, with visible chagrin. "You didn't have to wait."

"I know."

"That's, uh, that's great," she said, fumbling with her cigarettes. "Man, I'm dying for some pancakes."

Remy didn't say anything. He just sat there looking at her with those summer-rainstorm eyes, now green, now gray.

"Let's get out of here," Suzie said.

Remy got up without speaking and followed her out the door. They walked from the cabin to the main building mostly in silence, the air still humid, Suzie smoking, Remy walking alongside with his hands jammed in his pockets. Just outside the main building, Remy stopped and put his hand on Suzie's arm.

"Listen, Suzie," he said. "First of all, what you said was fucked up—"

"I'm sorry, I—"

"Let me finish. What you said was fucked up, but I understand that you might be a little stressed out right now. You probably feel vulnerable and—"

"I don't feel vulnerable, I—"

"Please," he said, holding his hands up, palms out in a gesture of peace and patience.

"Okay."

"You probably feel vulnerable and defensive. Okay. Let's just both recognize what you said and put it behind us for now. About everything else—I know last night was just a night. I had a lot of fun and I like you a lot, but we're both grown adults, and I can't let a hookup come between Jim and me, in our professional relationship." She stiffened, but he gave her a look, then went on, "And also you're also correct that it's none of his business whom I sleep with, or whom you sleep with, or if we sleep together. That is all one hundred percent valid, and a norm worth defending. Suzie, I can commit to you that if he tries to bring up what happened last night, ask about it, comment on it, he's going to have to answer to me, because that kind of talk is simply not appropriate." She exhaled smoke, listening. He went on, "What I would ask of you is to not provoke him. First of all, we hold the moral high ground on the issue now, but we lose it if we give him an excuse. Second, he's upset, and I suspect he'd be willing to remain upset, without pushing it, so long as we don't push it, either. Jim is a difficult man, but he's also, counterintuitively perhaps, rather passive. That's why he needs people around him, forces to bounce off of. Indeed, that's exactly why you're here. So what I would ask of you is to give him the space to be upset without engaging it. Don't push it. Don't give him something to bounce off of. Frankly, I believe once Jim gets used to the idea, he'll be fine. He is, whatever else he might be, a serious artist."

Suzie took a drag on her cigarette and looked up at the fragile blue-gray sky, imagining it shattering with the flick of a finger. "Like I said," she said, "I don't fucking explain myself to anybody. If he minds his own business, we're copacetic."

"Right," Remy said, not quite getting what he wanted, unwilling to push for more.

Suzie gestured at the door, cocking her head toward breakfast, and they went in to find the wedding party in the dining room chattering, sucking down mimosas, and shoveling eggs in their mouths. Jim had a table by the windows overlooking the lake, which shone flat glassy green in the morning light. He was drinking coffee and reading *USA Today* and looked up at them expressionlessly as they sat.

"Coffee?" he asked, holding up a teal carafe.

"Oh yeah," Suzie said, turning her cup over.

"I was just reading about the baseball commissioner fixing games," he said, waving the paper. "You believe that? They're saying the 2016 World Series was rigged. The Cubs! The Cubs! What the fuck?"

"That's fucked up," she said.

"I mean, okay, steroids and doping, whatever, it fucks shit up, it's a bit ridiculous, with the enhancements and supplements it's like these guys are like the Hulk or something. I mean it's unnatural." He glanced at Remy. "But they're still competing, right? I mean, if some guys do it, everybody does it, so it levels the field. It's still athletics. It's still a real competition. And, okay, if you want to suspend players for making political gestures, fine. Not democratic, but sport isn't democracy, right, it's a competition. So let them protest on their own time. But fixing games? Wow. Right?"

The waitress came up and asked them in a sugah-thick Oklahoma twang what they wanted, and they ordered eggs and bacon and pancakes, more coffee, and a large OJ for Suzie.

"So what's on the itinerary today?" Remy asked.

"What fascinates me is that he was involved with the mob, apparently," Jim said, looking at Suzie. "Some real bad sonsabitches. Real violent motherfuckers. I mean, there's so much money involved, they'd almost have to be, right?"

"Sure," she said, looking at Remy.

"What's on the itinerary, Jim?" Remy said again.

Jim folded his paper with an aggressive rustle. "What? You say something?"

"I asked what we had planned for the day."

"We," Jim said, gesturing between him and Suzie, "are gonna decide what *we're* doing, because Suzie's an equal partner on this excursion, as per her contract. *You* are gonna ride along and shoot what I tell you to shoot, as per your contract. Why? Did you have some suggestions from your research?"

"Well, Amarillo's coming up, and there's a lot of natural-gas fracking in the Panhandle."

"Sounds like maybe your research last night was a little scanty."

"I'm afraid I didn't get to it."

"Then what the *fuck* am I paying you for?" Jim laughed and looked at Suzie. "Hard to find good help these days."

Suzie didn't respond, and Jim let the silence draw out and fill the table. He looked back at Remy, staring him down.

"You two give me such a headache," he went on. "If it's not my writer contradicting every other thing I say, then it's my assistant slacking off on the job. But let's get back to the motherfucking *narrative*, aight? I was looking at this town in New Mexico called Trementina. It's only about five, six hours away. It's not even really a town. What it is, actually, is an underground Scientology fortress: Trementina Base. I want to get some footage there."

"Interesting," Remy said. "Can you see anything from the surface?"

Jim ignored him. "What do you think?" he asked Suzie. "Scientology, L. Ron Hubbard, armed fanatics hiding out in a bunker. Pretty weird, huh? Pretty American? I bet we could do some great kind of po-mo riff on that, something about nomad war machines, bodies without organs."

"I want to go to Altus," Suzie said, deadpan.

"Altus?" Jim said.

"Yeah," Suzie said. "I'd like to go see my parents in Altus."

"Uh, well, now, that sort of puts a crimp in our schedule, you know." Jim looked stricken. He tried to wave the idea away with a corner of the *USA Today*. "I was really hoping to make Albuquerque tonight, and if we go to Altus that's gonna put us almost a whole day behind."

Suzie warmed to the idea, which had surprised even herself. "Shit, Gene, it's only about half an hour from here. Plus, like you said, it's in my contract. I'll go talk to my parents, and y'all can film the pawnshops and massage parlors around the air base. It'd be perfect: military-industrial complex and all that shit. Read deal fucking nomad war machine, way better than some Scientology crap."

"I don't, uh, know. I don't know. Going back is against the whole thrust of the thing. The mission is to always keep moving forward."

"Yeah," Suzie said, "but I think it'd be good for you. There's a mythic aspect to the land, cowboys and Indians, I don't think you've really exhausted. I don't feel like you've even really explored it. I mean, where *are* your cowboys? Your Indians? I know you want to get to the desert, but I don't think you can really understand America until you understand Oklahoma."

"I think Suzie might be on to something," Remy said. "It would be a good chance to get some real people, as well. We've got a lot of footage of tourist sites, but we don't have a lot of people."

Jim's eyes blazed and the color rose in his neck. "You . . ." he started, then fell silent as the waitress approached with their food. After the plates were settled, Jim grabbed his fork and knife with a forced grin. "Alrighty, then. Altus it is."

But as they turned off the access road back onto 44, the plains around them a misty liquid bronze, Suzie found her stomach tightening and her mind succumbing to a frantic scrabbling anxiety. She could picture them rolling up the street, the old house growing larger as they closed in, and see her father standing faded and paunchy on the porch, holding his NINETY-SEVENTH AIR MOBILITY WING FIRST SERGEANT mug. He'd look at her through his hard and age-worn love with a disappointment barely distinguishable from disdain. And sitting next to him would be her mom, hair cut short, hands in her lap.

She knew what they looked like from the photos they sent with their Christmas cards. They'd tried to keep in touch for several years, but she'd limited contact to cards exchanged at Christmas. She couldn't let them in. Wouldn't. Every time they'd talked—and God, she'd tried—every time she was fourteen again, or eleven, or eight, scream-ing, livid, tearful. Every time they talked, her father was brusque and defensive, making her feel like he wanted to make sure she knew she didn't deserve his love, first because she was a girl, second because she was a fuckup, and third because she'd betrayed the very ideas of family, tradition, and discipline, the very Calder name, by going off to New

York and making a selfish, art-pretentious mess of her life. You're not tough enough, she heard him thinking, you don't understand loyalty, you don't understand sacrifice. Even her academic work in high school, Model United Nations and Biology Club, second place at state in track, none of it was enough. He wanted her in JROTC. He wanted her wearing wings. He wanted to see her fly.

Mom was just crazy: three miscarriages in a row, then finding out she couldn't have any more kids, which had been pretty much her only reason for living. The darkest years, Mom was the Joker to Dad's Batman, suicidal depressions followed by swings into mania, a week of relative stability, then a furious, screaming, crying explosion signaling another descent, days and weeks through which Mom would linger affectlessly, barely mobile. Suzie and Dad would cook dinner, clean up, tiptoe, not speak, each retreating to their own defenses. This was where she learned to read long novels. This is where she learned to make space inside a blank page, to listen for the harmonics speaking through her.

Puberty was where she learned to say fuck you. The hormonal charge erupted with a howl, and she discovered she could use her words to batter the world around her, the world that had trapped her into a dim room at the end of a silent hall. She got into fights at school, she made her teachers cry. No one knew what to do, but she started to get to know the kids in detention and soon found she couldn't talk to her dad without screaming. He resorted to threats of physical violence, but she knew better. Hit me, First Sergeant, she screamed, and I'll turn you in and they'll take me away and you'll lose your fucking job!

Mom just started coming out of the darkness then, thanks to some new pills, and it must have been like waking from one nightmare into another. As she attempted to resume her motherly duties, she found herself confronted by a foe who showed no mercy. The fact was, Suzie didn't recognize this woman meddling in her life; the only mom she'd ever known was the one who'd lived life sad. This new woman threatened everything. Lost in the waves of emotion, Suzie did what she could to make things right: she made her mother cry. She savaged her. She ignored and derided her, she fought and undermined, she piled on as much abuse as her father let her get away with, then more, leaving her mother blasted, addled, and afraid. The nightmare only ended when she left for college.

And now what? You think you can just start over?

The air in the car seemed to thin. Her lungs stopped working. Gray haze fuzzed the corners of the wilting sky. Suzie jammed the brake and yanked the wheel, pulling a U-turn in the middle of the highway, throwing Jim and Remy against their doors, the Valiant's tires squealing while behind them a driverless truck bellowed and swerved, almost running off the road. Headed north again, Suzie floored it and the Valiant leaped like a lion, roaring down the highway.

"What the fuck?" Jim shouted.

"Changed my mind," Suzie said, lighting a smoke and rolling down the window.

"What?"

"Lady's prerogative," she said. "Never mind Altus. Dumb idea."

"I thought you wanted—" Remy started from the back, but she cut him off.

"Fuck all that," she barked. "We head west. Start over. Just fucking start over."

The plains fade into dirt and scrub as they cross the Panhandle, passing Childress, Amarillo, and Glenrio, then rise into New Mexico, through Tucumcari, and turn off the interstate north. Mountains lift in the distance, a gray line of humps growing larger against the horizon, leviathans bobbing ponderously in their pod. The car's mostly quiet today, each actor settling into an individual holding pattern, accumulating haze. Five days on the road now and despite the drama they've got something of a routine, an established set of codes and prefixes. They know generally what's happening and what's expected. There's a bodily, animal pack-being, and they can sit together for miles in total silence. The road takes a meditative shape, the Valiant a still point on a rolling highway, the wide, wrinkled world around them and the hum of the wheels, and they find themselves lost in thought.

Or maybe they don't know what to say. Maybe the drama had upset things too much. Jim seemed closed in on himself, unwilling to engage, snappish, dark eyed. Remy, turning monkish and deferential, revealed that his ties to Jim were still stronger than any intimacy he'd established with Suzie. Suzie was shaken by the sudden plunge into memory, the unexpected turn to Altus and what seemed like a narrow escape, what was that Faulkner quote about the past? Or was it Joyce? Something something never wake up? She felt her hands moving through ghosts, the car driving through ghosts, her mind caught in a web of ghost voices, *I'm still your mother and you can't take that away from me* . . . She felt far, far away from Remy and Jim and the present, no longer caring about the game being played but feeling trapped in a lifetime's worth of bad decisions, trapped in a stupid car driving across a stupid fascist country.

She'd had to get out, she'd had to get out of Oklahoma and away, she'd had no choice—if she'd stayed or even just kept in touch they would have entangled her, strangled her, dragged her down into some state of being she couldn't be, something un-her, some anti-Suzie, for fuck's sake couldn't they see she didn't have a choice? It was a matter of survival. And from that initial no, which had been the only way she could see to say yes, things rolled out in a series of half-baked reckless zags, lunging through life as if in a drunken skid, trying to grab hold of something solid until, finally, battered back and forth between bad situations escaped from and lame fuckarounds she'd had to rise above, she found herself here, fucking one guy to fuck with another, getting paid to ride in a kitsch car and write bullshit, trapped in one more half-assed dodge, another too-dearly-bought moment of liberation from her precarious New York life, from Steve the Cat and her job and her so-called friends, her bullshit creative writing courses at the bullshit New School with all the other bullshit bullshitters, and this, too, what was this but a distraction and a fantasy? Even more than usual, because it was a vacation and had to end. No better than a fucking novel. It was the kind of temporary release we all seek, an unreality binge, the kind of release we seek from our daily life to make it bearable, a new show, an affair, an election, and now, realizing how far she'd come and how little ground she'd covered, she decided maybe it wasn't enough. Maybe a whole new something wasn't just a mythology they were deterritorializing, but something she needed to do, to find—break the pattern for real, really start over somehow real next time for real.

She watched the scenery roll by, the western horizon out the window flat like a line drawn through space, edged by distant purple angles. You could draw a line through anything, she thought, lighting a cigarette. You draw a line and a point and that's it, that's life, all the way into it.

Remy watched her from the back, watched her smoke in digits counting up through the camera, wondering what she was thinking. She must be deciding what to do, he thought, about Jim and me. Or maybe she's watching the dusty, wounded shacks by the road and thinking about her flyover girlhood in Altus. Or who knows, really, what people think, or if they even do, properly so called. Do any of us really? Think? Or do we just invent narratives ex post facto, rationalizations framing the act, explanations to make sense of the images we're left with?

Up ahead he saw a rusted neon sign stripped raw in the wind, reading WESTERN MOTEL. He turned the camera to track it going by.

"That's our sign," Suzie said, gesturing with her cigarette.

"What sign?" Jim asked.

"What the sign said. That's us."

"Huh? What are you talking about?"

Suzie smiled. "Don't worry, Gene. We're almost there."

"Sure," Jim said, perplexed. "Speaking of which, next time we stop, we need to get some sandwiches. I want to get to Trementina before the sun sets, which means we don't really have time to sit down and eat."

The desert rolled by like so much scenery.

They got shitty prepackaged sandwiches at the gas station at Conchas Dam, then drove to Trementina, where they pulled off the road near a sign that said DANGER NO TRESPASSING: AREA PATROLLED BY DRONE. Suzie took a nap in the car while Jim and Remy walked into the desert. The two men didn't really talk: they filmed and muttered to each other only as necessary. One time Remy tried to bring up Suzie, but Jim brushed it off. There wasn't much to see, and after about half an hour they were spotted by a drone. It hung in the sky watching them for ten minutes or so until a Scientologist pulled up in a Land Rover. He told them they had to leave or he'd have them arrested: he would drive them back to their car. He refused to turn on the air-conditioning. He refused to answer Jim's questions. When he dropped them off, he told them that some of their drones were patrol drones, but others were armed. "You were lucky this time," he said. "Don't try your luck again." Then he drove away. By that time it was getting late, so they decided to make a straight shot to the next hotel.

They hit Las Vegas, New Mexico, at around seven-thirty, and instead of taking I-25 north, Suzie took 518, heading up into the Sangre de Christos. She didn't ask, just made a decision and drove, and Jim didn't say anything. Then, past

Tres Ritos, she turned southwest toward Santa Fe, buzzing down through Peñasco, Truchas, and Chimayo, and finally stopping at the Cities of Gold Casino and Hotel in Pojoaque a little after ten.

"How many rooms should I get?" Jim asked.

Suzie gave him a dirty eyeball. "Three rooms, Jim. Like usual."

He nodded sagely. They got their rooms. Jim said "Happy trails" and went up. Suzie told Remy she was really tired and was gonna hit the sack. Remy got high and watched *Fort Apache* on cable.

In the morning, Jim was gone.

II. Roadhouse Blues

The only question on this journey is: how far can we go in the extermination of meaning, how far can we go in the non-referential desert form without cracking up and, of course, still keep alive the esoteric charm of disappearance? A theoretical question here materializes in the objective conditions of a journey which is no longer a journey and therefore carries with it a fundamental rule: aim for the point of no return. This is the key. And the crucial moment is that brutal instant which reveals that the journey has no end, that there is no longer any reason for it to come to an end. —Jean Baudrillard

Jack watches the road road and hums hums to himself and doesn't have to turn turn to see Jane Jane curled against the door asleep can feel her and hir feel Jane Jesse in the rearview rearview to check check on Jesse asleep under the camera recording road road and Jack's hard hard thinking of fucking Jane Jane later Jane Jesse fucking thinking fucking skin and saliva thinking fucking thinking whispers and teeth and he smokes a cigarette or doesn't or whatever's cool cool and in charge driving driving across the desert while they sleep dreaming dreaming of him or the road or the car car in a movie movie driving across the desert so hot so cool pure symbol all cowboy hat and dusty squint smoking smoking so cool so hot so fucking thinking fucking no filter all tar hums hums some hard-assed cheroot burning burns and reality burning fucking thinking driving a hundred percent death

Jack watches the road hums to himself and doesn't have to turn to see Jane curled against the passenger door asleep can feel her there but does glance now and again in the rearview to check on Jesse who seems to be meditating or sleeping sitting with hir eyes closed palms flat on hir knees hir chest rising and slowly falling again under the camera ze's left mounted in its bracket on the ceiling which Jack had to admit is getting some beautiful road footage of the desert the highway and the sky like the physical representation of pure thought and then Jack's thinking about thinking as he slips into the alpha wave of pure drive through forms drifting and nothing real nothing forgotten nothing remembered every path the slow throb of the car and he isn't thirsty and doesn't have to piss and isn't hungry or tired and the car's not riding the road but flying ever so slightly above it and he's not sitting but levitating over the leather and nothing connects to anything except through the idea of it like the car rides the idea of the road and the idea of riding and the car is an idea too and so is not-car and not-road and even not-Jack and not-Jane and not-Jesse and trinity and God and death and if he drove fast enough they'd fly off the planet into space not-space which is the idea of non-ideas so he drives faster and faster and faster and faster and faster and faster

One car rockets by then another, blasting the wall with light/humming in the dark/image of the road and sand and sun still and fading to silence.

Jack's hunched over the wheel bending the car into the future and Jane's halfway turned watching the chase in the rear. Jesse's in the back with the camcorder.

One car rockets by then the chase blasting the wall with light, swerves left into oncoming, gaining on them, clawing inches out the dial, needle wavering and sinking right, big numbers, big big numbers.

Cut to frontal shot chase car: two Russian faces in the windshield *Get them, Vladimir! They cannot get away from us this time!* One pulls a heavy automatic pistol from under his coat—no, he pulls a sawed-off from the footwell—no, he's got polonium in a vial—no, he turns and lifts an RPG out of the back seat and angles thru the window, perching his ass on the door, big rocket waving at the kids in the car ahead. Hot wind blows Russki goon hair. *Schas po ebalu poluchish, suka, blyat!*

Chrome and glass gleam in the sun. She's wearing sunglasses. He's in a white T-shirt, dungarees, and motorcycle boots. She's—ah—what? In a pale gray dress wide across wide hips and cone tits and her hair's up in a messy bun—no, no, she's in black capri pants and a loose white cotton blouse and a pageboy—no, no, she's in a Death Grips T-shirt and clunky hipster frames and cutoff jean shorts, barefoot, ponytail, smacking gum in candy-slick red lips. They're all in black and white except her candy-slick red lips. Jesse's 8mm whirs.

Jack, Jane says, they got a bazooka.

She's not like that at all. None of this is like that. She's in a flowery summer dress and bug-eye sunglasses and Scarlett Johansson hair. He's wearing green plaid pajama bottoms, Chuck Taylors, and a Team Hufflepuff hoodie. His hair's a muss, young Elliott Gould or maybe Michael Cera. Jesse's in a scarf, fiddling with hir iPhone 9.

Jack, Jane says, they have a bazooka.

What? he screeches, mugging for the camera. Cue laugh track.

Tracking shot, cut, cut back to the Russian pulling the trigger, sparks and light, rocket red bursts and arcs at them, but they slide out beneath the smoking spiral—it slams into the road, exploding, the chase squeals around the boom off across the sand, driver shouting—*Blyad!*—into the cacti.

Crazy kids speed into distance, safe now, and Jack says something dopey and Jane says something clever, sarcastic, contemporary.

Commercial comes screaming jump cuts, loud noises, product sex, cleaner, safer sex, yogurt sex, Diet Dr Pepper sex, more life. One after another, screaming jump cuts, loud noises, product sex, narrative sex, character, lifestyle, the morality of ends and means.

Dad shifts where he lies on the floor sleeping behind the

child cross-legged watching the lights flickering across the room/humming in the dark/commercials end and the show comes back on, image of the road.

I can't believe they snuck up on us like that, Jane says. You even see 'em?

They been following us since Michigan, says Jack.

Michigan! Why didn't you say anything? *Asshole!*

Look, sorry, I didn't wanna tip 'em off.

God, you're always like that. Like you always know best. Can you *please* not be such a fucking dick?

Yeah, okay, fine. I just thought you'd flip out, like you actually—

Flip out? *Flip out!?* You want me to flip the fuck out, you keep pulling this smart-guy routine. We've been doing this together too long for you to treat me like I just got here. In fact—

Look—

In fact—

Would you two just—

Rosy-lipped dawn kissed the canyon's edge, smearing it pink and bronze, while, still, all below rose and fell in a tumult of monochrome blue, a faded photo burning out along one edge studded with black burs, juniper, and creosote. It's rock, not sand, rock and a thin layer of cryptobiotic soil knotted like scar tissue ripped apart eons ago in long-forgotten geological holocausts, archaic renditions in Wingate sandstone dating to the Late Triassic, Cutler torn from the Early Permian.

Jim's breath caught: the *awesome grandeur*. No other words for it. Sweeping. Awesome. Spectacular. Awesome. Sublime. Sublime. Beyond human comprehension. Tasting the words on his tongue. A whole herd of men, a Grand Central Station riot of thousands, tens of thousands, a hundred thousand humans and their robot cars cascading over the plateau and off the edge, bodies falling in clumps and pairs and singles, would be the merest trickle breaking against the unyielding stone, a temporary organic bounty, water, carbon, and nutrients. That's how much we mean here, and even less. Even less because nothing was good to eat, water was scarce and usually poisonous. One saw here with undeniable lucidity that God had not made the earth for man, but to sate unknowable alien desires.

Jim already knew we were only animals, like polar bears or sea slugs, but the land before him cut to the bone of it, peeled back the skin of his species' existence. Man, woman, Republican, Democrat, artist, banker, cuck, bitch, none of it mattered here. You were a bipedal savanna primate, an animal caught in the open. You huddled squatting on the mesa in the morning chill, grunting like a chump, watching the sun come up and smoking one of Suzie's Parliaments as the red-orange curtain fell down the wall of the canyon and slowly faded, turning everything light.

A fox came up over the edge of the rise where he sat and crossed before him, upwind, unseeing. Jim inhaled smoke and the fox spun at the quiet burning crackle of paper and tobacco, tail level, curling on one plane as it hissed, narrow muzzle baring teeth. Then as quickly as it appeared it was gone, back over the edge of the rise. Jim thought again how glad he was he'd left Suzie and Remy at the hotel. The idea had just come to him, a clear solution, and he took it. The car had been weighing him down, the camera, the script, all that artifactual scaffolding. Art was reality and reality had no audience. Here was the thing itself: deep surface. This was it, this moment, not all that confabulation. Right now. This sentence. These three words.

Once the sun was fully up, he crammed his sleeping bag in its stuff sack and, lifting his carry-on, walked back the half mile to the highway, where he waited, thumb at the ready. He was passed by two semis, three SUVs, and a hatchback before an Indian in a pickup truck pulled over.

"Thanks," Jim said as he got in the cab.

The Indian was in his early sixties, a ropy, sunburned

workingman wearing at the edges. He wore a cowboy hat over a gray mullet. A Diné College parking pass hung from his rearview mirror.

"Ya'at'eh," he said. "Where you headed?"

Jim pointed up the road.

The man grunted. "How far?"

Jim put his hands up. "I'll be honest, man, I don't know. I'm just going."

"Okay," the man said, accelerating back onto the highway.

"I'm not gonna do anything, if you're worried," Jim said. "I'm just traveling. I'm not running from the law or anything."

The man smiled grimly. "Maybe you're the one oughta be worried."

Jim laughed. "Maybe I should. You gonna do something?"

"Naw," the man said. "Not if I don't need to. I'd scalp ya, but nowadays they just throw you in jail for scalping white boys. Not like the good old days, hey?"

Jim laughed again, and the old man's smile warmed.

"Tell you what," he went on, "I'm going as far as Monticello. Going to see my sweetheart. Now so long as you don't tell my old lady, I'll let you ride that far, okay?"

"Sounds good," Jim said. His heart felt light out here, riding these many miles. Everything was easy.

"You're a long way from nowhere," the Indian said after a minute. "You out camping?"

"Sort of, yeah."

"What's 'sorta' mean? I see you ain't got no backpack, just that rollie bag. You jump out of a plane somewhere?"

"I was on a trip with some people," he said, "and I decided

to split off on my own. Filling out the pattern required a kind of fractal divergence that wasn't possible at the level of collective meaning, and there was no way forward that didn't move right back into the cycle of reaction, because that particular system led only to certain end states, no matter how much turbulence you put into it. So in order to phase shift to the next level of emergent self-organization, I had to disrupt the socius not only at the level of semiotic production but also at the level of the real itself. The only way forward, as it were, was to break out of teleological progression altogether, which was impossible within that particular assemblage of affects and wills. I'm still on the trip; I just let them keep the car. Long story short, I'm making a movie."

The Indian nodded. "A movie, hey? Where's your camera?"

"Right here," Jim said, tapping his mirrorshades.

"Those Google glasses?" the Indian asked, suddenly suspicious.

"No," Jim said. "I mean me. My eyes. I'm the camera. Reality has no audience."

"Eyyyy," the Indian said, relaxing. "Pretty clever. So what's your movie about, hey?"

"It's about America and the idea of starting over and the problem of narrative, the way we get trapped in stories, the stories we tell ourselves. It's about revolution and utopia and climate change and violence and guns and the Civil War and cowboys and Indians and space. *Homo sapiens*, the greatest of apes, mere geology. It's points, lines, and space. It's about me and you and all this."

The wheels thrummed on the blacktop. The La Sal Mountains rose purple and gray in the distance. The Indian took a drink from his giant plastic travel mug. "So how's the movie end, hey?" he asked.

"That, my friend, is the million-dollar question. Because it's the end that makes the story, right? I mean, the difference between comedy and tragedy is all in the punchline. A wedding or a death? A bang or a whimper? Laughing or crying? I don't know. All I know is I have to keep going until the end finds me."

"You got no plan, then?"

"Nope. I had one, before this, but then . . . I was planning too much. I had to do this and that and the other, and it was all getting very rigid. Too binary, too dialectical. I had to get rhizomatic again. The essence of the road movie idea, see, is in transgressing the normative constraints on our choices, breaking through negation to total autonomy, but as long as I kept sticking to the plan, the algorithm kept getting locked into a feedback loop. Suzie taught me that, weirdly enough, with Altus. I realized that conflict works against the whole idea. Planning works against the whole idea. Form itself is the problem. I had to, you know, derange myself. Disrupt the program."

"You sure you ain't on drugs, hey?"

"Just tobacco," Jim said. "I haven't even had any coffee."

"Well, there's coffee there in the thermos by your feet. You help yourself."

"Thank you. Ah, thank you—?" Jim held out his hand.

"Marvin," the Indian said, shaking Jim's hand.

"Thank you, Marvin. My name's Jack."

"Nice to meet you, Jack. Hope your movie turns out all right. Maybe you give me a screen credit, ey, like Third Indian from the Left."

"Absolutely," Jim said, unscrewing the cup on top of the thermos, resting the cup on his knee, then unscrewing the top of the thermos and pouring coffee into the cup. "I have to say, it's all going pretty well right now. What kind of town is Monticello, anyway? You think I can get a backpack there?"

"Nope, I don't reckon you can get no backpack in Monticello. But you can probably catch a ride to Moab and get you one there, at Pagan Mountaineering or Gearheads. Them are both right on Main Street." Marvin hawked and spit out the window. "Tell you what, you sure picked some rough country to hitch through, Jack. You're really taking your life in your hands."

"It's all right," Jim said. "I don't have anything else to do now but wait, watch the road, and make my movie. Another ride always comes along."

I'm a wild drifter, see, a real cool customer living on the edge. I roll into town like I got nothing to lose, and that's when I see her there in the diner, popping bubblegum like she's breaking hearts.

I say, "Baby, you and me, we'd go a long way together," and she says, "Honeylamb, you don't even know what kinda *fire* yer playing with."

So I grab her and kiss her and show her my tattoo. She says she never could say no to a guy in a cowboy hat, so we take off into the sunset.

Everything would've turned out fine, too, if'n it hadn't a been for that state trooper. I didn't like the way he looked at Jane, the way her legs shone in his mirrorshades, and then he started sticking his nose into questions like where I got the car.

Jane calmed down after a while, and I pulled off and parked around the back of a Cracker Barrel, where I could wash the blood out and nobody'd look too close. We'd gone off the rails, I could feel it, damned and doomed American outlaws, two kids living on the edge, dancing in the fire, crazy living, crazy life full of blood and sex magic and hard drugs. Damn that dead cop, though, 'cuz he got his revenge: his chest camera caught us tighter than any roadblock, locked down red-handed in the flicker, and they lit up the web coming after us with every drone they had.

Ain't nobody love a cop killer no more, not since the globalists took over the Deep State and poisoned everybody's minds with their blue-pill propaganda. Thing is, people seem to want it. I mean, they take the pill. I reckon folks is just scared of real freedom and tired of the burden of individuality, the weight of having to choose a self, be a self, forge a self from the detritus of consumer society's endless maelstrom of bullshit.

Anyways, from then on it was a mad, bloody, octane-fueled blaze up to Ol' Canada. We left everything we owned behind us, dirty socks dumped in rest-stop trash cans, old underwear left in the greasy sinks of two-pump gas stations, phone chargers spun like baby snakes curling in the Arizona sand, condoms jammed in ATM money slots, birth certificates folded into Chinese menus, phones left on the tables of truck-stop diners, credit cards scattered like a shot cheater's poker deck, watches melted in the dashboard sun, skin and eyes and teeth shred in crackling folds, buried in a dumpster behind a Shell on Route 315, everything but everything until all we had left was memories, and them we burned for fuel. I never thought we'd make it, but all I knew was that me and Jane was all we had . . . It was us against the world, our one and only trueborn chance to start over.

The clouds come over and the heat shudders with the scream of cicadas. The crunch of gravel under tires. Hardly even a town, just a few old buildings peeling paint, the hotel, the church, the granary, a feed store, hardware store. Some nice old houses that once meant the world to somebody, now boarded and empty, or maybe the lights come on but it's just some old couple, a man retired and his wife, or maybe their middle-aged daughter and her family, a woman with ovarian cancer, a man with a cleft palate and a scar across his forehead. You had to believe some day in the past boys in dark jeans with turned-up cuffs rolled hoops down the lane with sticks, laughing and playing, while girls double Dutched, two ropes flickering one inside the other. You had to believe because now there was nothing, no children, no life, and to think it was always like that, like it had never had a future even on the day it was built, would be too much.

The hotel stands back off the main street, on a gravel road, with an empty field to one side. It's a simple, square two-story box with the word HOTEL painted over the door. She couldn't imagine who might have stayed there in this nowhere town besides maybe traveling salesmen, itinerant preachers, and suicides.

Next to the hotel was an open garage where a thick man with pomaded hair stood in his overalls watching. He had a burgundy 1960 Impala parked in the grass, all lines and fins, a long cigarettey machine. Later she dreamed

Gone and where. They, he. Stained on stone.

Green pines, red rock, men and women stained on stone. Gone and where. Verb.

She lifted her hands to touch the bodies, limbless souls floating up, up, up, then held back thinking of her skin oil on the stone, staining it, the admonition from the pamphlet, the idea of how many thousands of years gone, then she had to touch it, feel the connection with the dead, whatever cost, whatever prohibition.

Gone and where.

The strangest thing was he left the car in the lot and the keys at the desk, along with his production-company credit card. Like it was an invitation.

They lay together in the camp tent, Remy with his hands rebuffed, her staring up through the mesh vent to see the stars while he, turned away, tried to make her feel his frustration through the tension in his back.

She was bored with this now, with Remy, with driving, now that Jim was gone. What did that mean? Anything?

They weren't going to find him, she knew that, and Remy's insistence that they search never seemed totally honest. Did he know something? Was it a trick?

She thought of the figures on the canyon wall, the ledge, from earlier that day, the men and women stained on stone, and it made her dizzy to think of them living here in the sand and rock so long ago. What water did they drink? How did they . . . anything? It was an image of our future, she thought: two by two, wandering through an empty desert, slowly drying to stone. The last cannibals.

Going back to New York already sounded like the right idea, and soon would become necessity. And then what? Try to find some new life built on repudiating the one before, wait for the end of the world. Easy enough. Plenty of practice. The freedom she'd tasted out here on the road was good, but it was a freedom of rootlessness and dust. It was the freedom to be blown and scattered, which was never the freedom she sought even if it was the only one she'd ever found.

How had they lived here, the pictograph people? In huts? In caves?

What did they eat?

How. How much. How? As if life were a line you could cut into, an animal you could carve limb from limb, bones you could crack to get at the marrow inside. Is the word discontinuous or discrete? She wondered. Am I making that up? You can't separate out the things that go together. You can't cotton to the fact that time and space are the same space, the same thing, that space and space and space are the same space. One time, one space, one thought, but we chop it all up. Two different thoughts at the same time differ neither in time or space, so how do they differ? In content? Form? In different strobing sectors of the cerebellum? So you will, in the end, say space, yes, space, different cells and chemical romances. Deferring unification.

This light, words careening inside a car. False. Holding two opposed notions, but how? Do I think them differently? What if they're not thoughts at all, but only afterimages of things that already happened? Rationalization of biorhythm.

She remembered his aggressive, fearful eyes. The twitch in his lip. She pictured him by the side of the road, standing on the shoulder, thumb out, going where? Gone and where? Why? Some kind of ploy? Is he gonna call them up and tell them come get him?

Remy seemed to think it was four-dimensional chess; he refused to believe Jim had gone plumb loco and lit out for the hills, the dark in-between, the tarp under the bridge. But that, Suzie held, was exactly what Jim wanted.

No, in fact, this was not the time for facts. Things happen and they flash across your brain, leaving images that form as words. Words happen, leaving images that flash across your brain, more words.

She was dreaming all of it: A little story about Jack and Jane and Jesse. An epic nightmare fantasy of the Donald and Taylor Swift and *Call Me Caitlyn*. Where did MS-13 fit in? And Kim Jong-Un? She was dreaming Kokopelli and Bonnie and Clyde. She was dreaming Charlie Starkweather and Caril Fugate and how they drove all the way out until the cops got them, and why did she do that? How? Gone and where? Dreaming different people, her old agent Anna, her horse-riding friend from Oklahoma named Grace, her mother, America, the children she might have had, the children she'd aborted, Jack and Jane, puppets dancing, playing out scenarios on the inner wall of her mind in shadows cast by the false light of consciousness, because that's what Suzie does, has always done. She doesn't take reality as it comes, but pumps it through a machine in her head that spits it out as stories she can control. Stories that make some kind of sense. Stories that hold at a distance the horror of being trapped in a box made of words, nightmare mind—look ma, no hands.

She wishes she could break the machine, stop it from making stories, stop it from always starting over. She wishes she could lie on the floor of the world and stare up at the stars, a word comes in, goes out, gone and where. Nowhere. They, he. When. Float. Stone. Words come in and out, but nothing ties them together, like stars unconstellated, each one shimmering distant, isolate, bright.

Jack and Jane had been driving all night when the bricks fell, cascading, the bricks didn't fall. Go back and read it again. Skip the next sentence. We are caught in nets of envy. The back seat full of crumpled wax too lazy to throw a gray pill of cigarette ash arcing under the windshield like a ballerina. Wait for it.

Something happens it always does. They watch hotel TV all night. They watch paintings of wildlife: caribou, acrylic. They watch one another, blue light glowed skin, blood seething in static horizontals, eyeball tire tracks. They met the man who wrote the algorithm for the French & Indian War. They met a man who played dead.

They arranged figures on a table reenacting the death of John Henry, still but for the machine. Blades whispering. Gravel crunches underfoot.

Read gravel crunch foot. Underfoot? Read shadows. The ice clatters in the ice machine. The whole system lurches and pixels grind. It's nice there's an ice machine. Also a Coke machine and a snack machine with Honey Buns, Twizzlers, and chili cheese Fritos. Everywhere the comforts of home.

How he remembers the gravel underfoot, old Jack, and it brings back the taste of dust and the crisp, smoky dusks of autumn. Fields burning. It brings back and blows down.

Water in all its forms, rising. Breathe. Breathe in. I can't breathe.

Jack and Jane fold like matches struck over the back of the cover and Mom puts the kettle on, Dad plays "Imagine" in loafers, cars everywhere drip light down blackening walls. More water/nets. Nets like highways, like water. They met a man who taught them to code.

The highways are red like we know and. No and. Start over.

Cars everywhere drip light down gray walls, ashen walls, monochrome walls, mercurochrome walls, walls the color of holocaust pictures, faded walls, deliberately distressed walls clawhammered to look older than they are, the light sliding again and again and one more time in schiz, blob, and reel, pooling in a slick on the floor leaking down the street, filling our kitchens with water. The highways are red, are blazing. No. There are no highways only the sea the map.

He erases his name and writes it again. I can't breathe.

Jane stands over Jack and lays a cold brick on his chest. He looks at her, her fingers still. She pushes down and he breathes in, his ribs lifting, filling his cage with air, and she pushes harder. His heart beats, she can feel it in her fingertips rough with red grit dust. She straddles him and leans, both palms against the stone, until he can't inhale any farther. He holds his breath, looking into her eyes, as his sight goes dim. He exhales. His chest sinks and with it the brick, in through the skin, blood folding bone around rock.

Outside a horn sounds, inside breathing. The highways are black like a line across the sky. The sea. No zero.

You ask, at a certain point, what it's all about.

La Iglesia de la Virgen de los Remedios: the white cross in the mountain clearing between pines green and dark.

The crashed car down the road: they ran on the flat as long as they could, till the rim gave out and they ditched. Jane pulled herself from the car, bleeding in the side from where they got her, and started limping, gun heavy in her hand, looking back over her shoulder, sunglasses glinting in the high mountain blaze. They'd stopped the last one, but it was only a matter of time.

Jesse dead in the back. Plugged in the chest and gut, ze didn't last long. Jack, meanwhile, shirt wrapped around his head to stanch the blood, is mumbling "Jane, Jane" as he pushes open the door and falls, legs collapsing. It's getting dark now for Jack. The sun doesn't seem to work like it used to.

"Jane," he gasps, face in the needles, trying to push himself up with his knees. Gotta give him credit for trying.

Jane legs it up the road, each step a jab in her side. Liver? Uterus? Stomach? Or maybe she's lucky and the bullet went right through. Either way it's tearing her insides up and she needs help, she knows that much. Fuck pain.

Up ahead she sees the church and the huge white cross

behind it in the clearing, the smaller cross in the gravel. Read gravel crunch foot.

Had to end somewhere. There's no way this crazy spree could have lasted forever—and did we even really *want* to make it to Canada? Did we even think we could do that?

She thought back on the ride, the first bold revolt, the thrill when she crossed the threshold and shouted: "This is the resistance." The excitement she felt the first time she pointed her gun at someone, the shudder of sexual pleasure when it went off, the grace of falling bodies. The beauty of a dead cop.

But everything comes to an end, and that was the point anyway. A new beginning needed an end to start over, burn, burn, never fade away.

She can hear the sirens, cruisers on their way up the dusty track. Only a matter of time.

Her tank top soaked with blood and sweat now, she'd never realized what hard work it was to die. She felt her back pocket for extra mags—three, at nine rounds each, meant twenty-seven plus the five or six in the gun. Against however many cops, pistols, shotguns, Homeland, SWAT, ATF, DEA, and the FBI. You think maybe they brought the National Guard? For little ol' me?

A puff of dust down the mountain at the turn. She can see only the black MRAP in front, with the water-cannon cupola. Maybe they'll stop at the car and think that's it. Except there's an APB for one man and two women (patriarchal sexist cis-het fucks), armed and dangerous. This was it. This was really it.

She threw herself against the door of the church and

slammed it open. Up near the altar a young priest looked
at her, his face calm even as she raised her pistol. Sitting
before him, her back to the door, a huddled pile of bones
and white hair draped in a Yavapai poncho, a woman so old
she might have seen Cortez burning his ships.

"Padre," Jane rasped. "I need a little remedios."

He looked at her silhouetted against the brightness outside, hearing the sirens down the mountain, eyes on the
glint of pistol weaving in the doorway.

"Come in," he said, patting Quintana Juanita Alonzo
Varga y Lopez Pretty-on-Top's shoulder and leaving her sitting in the pew. "I'll return, tía," he whispered to the old
woman as he moved toward the door.

Jane stepped in and closed the door behind her and
leaned against it. She stood slack for a moment, her gun
hand falling to her side and her head drooping, eyes losing
focus. She started to slide down the door, then with a grunt
and gritted teeth stood and stumbled toward the priest. She
growled, pulling herself together, breathing hard through
her nose.

He showed her the palms of his hands, trying to calm
her. "You're hurt very bad." The sirens louder now, nearly
on them. "I can help you. Just put down the gun."

"There any other way out of this place?"

"No, m'hija. You go out the same way you come in. *Mira,
hija*, I can help. Just put down the—"

"Only way you can help me now, Padre, is over my dead
body. You and the old woman better find some cover. This
is bound to get messy." Sirens blaring now, scatter of gravel,
the sky turned to blood.

"This is a place of God, *m'hija*," he said, almost begging.

"It oughta do, then." She pushed past him and up to the altar, with the Jesus of the Mount on one side and Mary of the Immaculate Heart on the other, and the suffering Christ himself hanging emaciated from his fierce crucifix between. It was a nice stone altar, very old school, almost heathen, and she could bend on one knee behind it and plug away all day as safe as if she was sitting in a bunker. She let herself down slow, her bloody right hand smearing the stone, then took up a supported stance on one knee, eyeing the doorway.

"*M'hija*, please," the priest said, "let me help."

"Might wanna help yourself the fuck outta the way, Padre," she said, sighting down the barrel.

Just then the door swung open and one cop came in low, another high, armored and helmeted, with carbines. The one going low had enough time to say "There—" before Jane put two in the crotch of the big beefy fucker standing up, just under his vest plate. Then, exhaling slow, she blew out the knee of the crouching one. The door erupted in splinters and fire, and the priest jerked and spun, caught in a swarm of lead.

"You're surrounded," came the voice over the bullhorn. "There's only two ways you come out of there, Suzie, in handcuffs or in a bag. It's up to you. You come out now with your hands up, we might even get you to a hospital."

"My name's not fucking Suzie!" she screamed, then winced at the pain in her side.

"This is your last chance," the bullhorn barked.

Maybe that's it, then, a bad end to a bad ride. If there's no fucking point to anything anyway, you might as well go down blazing.

"Come get some, you Trump-lovin' bitches," she shouted, the screen going dark.

Jack stood against the rear fender in the sun staring into the trees going up the hill across the highway, the road still rumbling in his ears despite or maybe because of the silence, this wide spot, this flytrap log cabin advertising HOME MAID LEMONAID and FRESH APPEL PIE'S.

Hey, she said. Why don't we call it a day?

Jack made a face.

Serious, Jane said from the back seat, looking at her phone. There's a creek and a lake and a park. Let's get a tacky room in a dirty motel where there's an oil painting of a deer on the wall, buy a couple six-packs, and take the rest of the day off. We'll go down to the creek and chill.

Two rooms.

You still upset about that?

What do you think?

I think we're all friends here.

We can make it to the border. Why stop now?

It's like six hundred miles.

We could be there by midnight. One, two at the latest.

You wanna drive for the next twelve hours? Through these mountains, in the dark? We're not gonna make it.

Jesse came out of the cabin carrying something small.

Hey kids, ze said, they got a stuffed bear in there. It's appalling. We should take pictures.

You wanna take the afternoon off? Jane asked.

Jesse opened the packet in hir hand and poured spicy peanuts in hir mouth.

Yeah, sure.

There you go, Gene. Two to one. You are *vetoed.*

Jack stared at her reflection in the rearview mirror, her bug-eye sunglasses staring back, blank slabs of shade, her phone in her hand, smooth lips slack and unyielding, then twisting and grinning, halfway malicious and halfway entreating, c'mon, don't be such a Krampus, ain't no thang. Or that's what he thought she thought. That's what he wanted to think she thought, but in fact she is to him a cipher, pure form, her words never connecting to reality the way other people's did, the way his or Jesse's did, for example, her actions occurring for motivations impenetrable from this dimension, her whole being shifting as if her mind were controlled by an alien intelligence who learned to be human from reading the backs of cereal boxes. What was she at? How long could this last? What did it really matter, in the end, whether or not they made it to Canada?

Or at least that's what he thought he thought. Jesse got it all on film. And nothing mattered anyway, not out here in Deadwood, out where it was happening.

Why don't we just do it in the road?

What?

Trucker sex, Jesse said. I like it.

Although, Jane said ruefully, they'd probably call the sheriff on us.

Let's go see that bear, said Jack.

Jane unfolded from the car, taking pictures with her phone. Is it a boy bear or a girl bear? she asked.

Your heteronormative gender binaries only serve to substantiate the political ontology of neoliberal patriarchy, Jesse said.

But does it have a dingus? Jane asked.

That's all you care about, isn't it?

Real talk, lover, Jane said, taking pictures of Jesse.

It's a mama bear.

You check?

No dingus.

Not the kind of motel where you get a robe; just pray the towels are clean. Jesse slid Jane's arm off hir, got up, pulled on a pair of shorts and a T-shirt, and washed hir face in the sink.

Jesse? Jack said.

Mhmhm?

You all right?

I'm just going for my "Continental breakfast."

What time is it?

Seven.

Fuck.

Jesse came back and looked sweetly at the two of them lying in bed.

You and Jane want anything?

She's still sleeping.

Shh, Jane hissed. I'm still sleeping.

That's all right, Jack said. I'll be out in a minute. Queen Mab needs her beauty sleep.

Shhhhh, Jane hissed. I'm sleeping.

Jesse nodded and left. Jack watched the door shut behind hir, then stared at the TV's blank screen, a gray square with white squares reflecting the morning light in through the curtains. He looked over at Jane sleeping beside him, her naked body sprawled under the bunched sheet.

He remembered it was September 11. He remembered it was the Fourth of July. He remembered it was Victory Day in Moscow, and Cinco de Mayo too. He remembered it was his birthday.

Would they have complimentary copies of *USA Today* in the lobby? He doubted it. Likely only a TV, if that. He imagined the sensual pleasure—if it *was* pleasure—of a bowl of Sugar Smacks poured from a single-serve box, a cup of whatever it was they'd call coffee, a multicolored pie chart showing the results of a Gallup poll.

Maybe they'd drive through Gallup today. Maybe they'd settle in Gallup.

He ran his hand along the sheet over Jane's hip and down her thigh, then back along and down the valley. Jane hissed and turned.

I'm sleeping, she said.

Jesse sat in back, aiming the camera at Jane's head, wisps of hair come unstuck over the auricle's helix and the vulnerable skin at the nape of her neck.

I hear they're using napalm in Sinaloa, Jack said.

Jesse watched Jane's head cock slightly toward Jack, then swing back past its original position to the right, so now the shot's the whole back of her head.

In the age of the Anthropocene, she read, history and biology seem to converge.

Just like in Vietnam, Jack said.

Jane shook her head, then went on reading. The consequences of rapid—in brackets—microbial—close brackets—reproduction coupled with differences in evolutionary strategy is that the microbial part of us evolves more rapidly than the non-microbial part of us and can respond more quickly to environmental changes. That a part of us might be capable of coping with more acidic water, wilder weather, and higher temperatures than other parts of us produces a strikingly different version of what might be endangered. Understood in this way, quote—the body multiple—close quotes—is not an italicized entity to be protected but an italicized system, an interactive process of life and death combined.

Jane read on: The soup of synthetic chemicals in which we now live puts human masculinity—I like that, she interjected, quote human masculinity unquote—at risk and affects reproduction in wildlife worldwide. Just to take a few of the most startling examples provided by Nancy Langston, quote Male alligators exposed to DDT in Florida's Lake Apopka developed penises that were one-half to one-third the typical size, too small to function, ellipses. Prothonotary warblers in Alabama, sea turtles in Georgia, and mink and otters from around the Great Lakes all showed reproductive changes. Male porpoises did not have enough testosterone to reproduce, while polar bears on the Arctic island of Svalbard developed intersex characteristics. End quote. Surveys of many British streams discovered that quote more than thirty percent of the fish ellipses are now intersex. End quote.

Jane turned to look at Jack. Jesse watched her zygomatic arch, the folds of skin at the lateral palpebral commissure, her smooth mandible line and complicated, tender commissure of lip. Ze focused and unfocused, shifting to pure color, pale pinks and darker smudges, in and out of time.

At the usually less-than-toxic levels at which every person today is suffused with industrially manufactured substances, Jane read, it is hard to imagine that there are not subtle, em dash, and perhaps not so subtle, em dash, changes in our thought processes and emotional responses. If history involves self-reflection yet the self has been chemically altered, how do we proceed? How would we even be able to measure these effects, given the wide range of human abilities and different individual susceptibilities to chemicals. In asking these questions, we emphasize what we may be losing in terms of historical continuity and human solidarity, and also what neither we nor biochemists yet understand. New paragraph. On the other hand, if we italicized are our chemically altered environment, then who is the quote we endquote endangered by the industrial processes producing climate change? From this perspective, there may be no endangerment.

What kind of napalm? Jesse asked.

They didn't say, Jack said.

On who?

The resistance. Or maybe the Russians. I don't know. Same-same. The bad guys. What's the difference?

It makes a difference.

What difference?

Jesse put hir hair back and knelt on the macadam in the weird light, fiddling with the camera to catch the vacant browns and grays. Bolts of sun shot out of clouds, then cut off. Wind. Mind. Sky. Dust.

Ze pushed a button, texted Jane.

"Action."

for the law only.

*THis is For THE cops or LAW-
mEN who FiNES us. Caril
aND i arE wRiTing This so
That you and EVER body wiLL
Know what has happEM.
On tue. day 7 days befor
you have seen the bodys
of my mom, dad and baby
sister, these dead because
of me and chuck, chuck
came down that tue. day
happy and full of joke's but
when he came in mom
said for him to get out and
never come back, chuck
look at her, "and said why."
at that my dad got mad
and begin to hit him and
was pushing him all over*

*the room, then chuck got
mad and there was no
stoping him, he had his
gun whit him cause him
and my dad was going
hunting, well chuck pull*

it and the came out
and my dad drop to the
foor, at this my mom was

so mad the she had a
and was going to cut him
she knot the gun from
chucks hand, chuck just
stood there saying he was
sorry he didn't want to
do it. i got chucks gun
aND STOP MY MON FRON
KiLLiNg ChucK, BETTY

Jean was yelling so loud
i hit her with the gun about
10 times she would not
stop chuck had the

so he was about 10 steps from
her, he let it go it stop
some where by her head.
me and chuck just look
at then for about 4 HRS.
then we wrapped them and

pull them out in the house
in back.
mY SiSTErs AND EVEV ONE
ELES WE NOT BELIVED This
BuT iT's The TRUE AND
i Say it By gOD
then me and chuck

live with each other and
monday the day the bodys
were found, we were
going to kill our selves
But BOB VON BRUCK and
every body would not stay
a way.
and hate my older sister
and bob for what they are
they all ways wanted me
to stop going with chuck
show that sorry kid bob
Kwen could go with me.
chuck and i are sorry
for what we did, but now
were going to the end.
i feel sorry for Bar. to
have a ask like bob. over

I and Caril are sorry for what
has happen, cause I have
hurt every body cause of it

and so has caril. but i'm
saying one thing every
body that came out there
was lucki there not
dead even caril's
sister.

Chuck S
Caril F
x
so far we have Kill
7 persons.

"Stop here," Jane says.

"What's here?"

"Just stop."

Jack pulls the Valiant over and leaves the engine running. There's nothing here, just three boarded-up two-stories in a row with lawns growing wild like peewee jungles, then a three-story brick cube with fading paint across the top reading WESTERN HOTEL. A dying oak across the street defines an empty lot.

Jane pulls her .38—no, she reaches into her bag and whips out a .357 Magnum—no, she draws a Colt .45 Single Action Army revolver, pulled from the dead hand of Lieutenant William Van Wyck Reily at the Battle of the Little Bighorn by the Arapaho who cut him down, jams it in Jack's face, and cocks the hammer back.

"What the fuck?"

Jesse in back lowers the camera. "Hey, Jane," ze says.

"I got one question, Jack."

"Hey, Jane, it's all good," Jack says. "Just put the gun down. Little help, Jesse?"

"Jesse, you pick that camera back up and get this on film."

Which ze does.

"Jane, really—" Jack says.

"Shut up, Jack," she says, taking his chin and sliding the barrel of the Colt into his mouth. "I just need to know one thing, a simple yes or no. Carefully."

"Hohay," Jack says around the steel. "Hohay."

"Whose story is it?"

"Wha?"

"What?" Jane says back, smiling.

"Wha?" Jack says again, eyes wide.

"Wrong answer, motherfucker," Jane says, shaking her head, and pow, the top of Jack's head disintegrates out the window and there's blood and bone and brains all over. Sticky black red pouring out of the cave in his skull, so Jane reaches past him, pulls the handle that opens the door, and kicks him into the street. Good thing the window was open.

"You get that?" she asks Jesse as she slides over to the driver's seat. She looks around for a napkin to wipe up the blood.

"Fuck, Jane," ze says. "That's fucked up."

"You got it, right?"

"Yeah, but, Jesus . . . What now?"

Jane closes the door and holsters her Colt. The smell of cordite and blood is making her frisky. "Whyn't you hop in the front seat, lover," she says.

As they pull away, headed back out of the dry, dying nowhere they'll remember forever as Jack's Last Stand, Jane wonders if maybe there's a special heaven for the wholly pure, a place for people who never relented, never gave an inch, those who held to their standard of truth no matter what the cost, no matter what the truth. There orta be, she thinks, because in the end the only thing that mattered was whether you had a code.

Let's start over, he said, tapping nails on the table. Go out West and make a clean breast of things.

A clean break, she said, turning back to the counter.

Whatever.

The pads of her fingers on Formica. The yellow-lit ceiling of the tunnel. The smell of engine grease, a slickness like rippling eels. What could she say? Her hair frizzed with static and she zapped everything she touched.

Jesse II looked out past the rim of hir bowl at the rain and kicked hir feet. Dad scribbled blue circles across pink lines on yellow paper. Mom opened a cupboard and closed it.

What's out West? she said. In the other room Jesse I changed the channel, and they heard the TV say the police shot the woman four times.

Jesse II watched the red edge of hir bowl slip out of focus against the gray truck parked across the street slick with rain, what out West, what wasn't here, four times, the smell of grease, Jesse II watched the gray truck parked across the street slip out of focus against the red edge of hir bowl, the memory of teeth cracked porcelain, the taste of blood tongue, thick tongue, the taste of pig tongue. Jesse II watched the slip fog gaotack wall fuck nit. flt 7 sptik. jmmy jmny jmimy jmny. sk'k. Everybody hands up, hands flat on flat surfaces, fingers flat, all their pink and white fingers flat but for Jesse I in the other room whose paint-sticky, sweaty red digits twitched balled in fists bunched in the wool of hir sweater. And the rain fell, spattering against the windows and the cars and the street like old fat. Jesse II watched the rain slip the scene

should be dramatic, humming with portentous buzz. It smells like engine grease and old coffee. Everything is muted from the colors to. Stand the colors to. Can you mute a woman's backing her way out of life's assorted? Mute a man's sense of hope at the edge of risk, a gamble he's not sure he's got the balls to make, and the knowledge that she's lost faith? Can you mute her loss of faith? Or is it only momentary, just doldrums, seasonal affective whatever, and don't we have to just get through, for the kids or whatever, for life, just deal with it? Keep moving forward?

Dad's name is Jack. Mom is Jane. They're the J Crew. Smile. They go to Olive Garden on Sunday evenings and make it back in time for *The Walking Dead*. They have a tangible socioeconomic reality evoked by a combination of telling details and artfully crafted omissions. Dad drives a Prius.

If we go to California, Jesse II asked, do I have to go to school?

Yes, Dad said.

Can I go to one of those Muslim schools?

What?

Where they teach the Bible.

Muslims don't read the Bible. They read the Koran.

Yeah the Koran.

No, you can't go to Muslim school.

Can I watch TV then?

Mom opens the cupboard and turns on the screen. Dad pushes a button on the wall, the window flickers, static gray, resolving into to a D—— D—— cartoon. Mom slides her eyes from their sockets cutting loose the projecting beam, firing TV at the walls, the ceiling, TV piercing the table. The focus. The cereal bowl. Light on skin on light. Mom and Dad waltz the kitchen, singing "The Surrey with the Fringe on Top," don't you wish y'd go on forever, and Jesse I prances in, shooting hir Colt into the ceiling, hotfooting a flippetyflop jumparoo. What are you gonna do about it, that's what I'd like to know.

Deeper into the mystery, I saw then why Jack liked to have things very clearly organized. If they were really going out West, it would start an almost uncontrollable avalanche of signification. Speed of space. skintification. Spk'hhh. Can you imagine potato-chip bags slick inside with the grease of salty fingers, mustard packets, an inch of stale Cherry Coke at the bottom of a lukewarm, crumpling wax-paper cup? Can you feel Mom itching her scalp, her eyes weary with the same broken road, the same humming engine, the same stabbing whine, the same glance at Jack to make sure he's awake, make sure he's awake, make sure he's awake. We touch too much maybe

you should try a new shampoo let's

start

oh, what a beautiful

Mom buys a pack of Winston Lights on the sly and smokes

one out behind the hotel. Purple slabs of granite heave at the horizon, a wall of rock in which somewhere stands the gate the candy-apple-red semis keep rolling through, somewhere the way through, the western path. Dad changes channels upstairs while Jesse II looks out the window and writes in hir Dinosaur Journal. Jesse I—who knows? The sense of danger and novelty has faded into scummy unconcern, the apathy of open space. Clouds point this way and that, no clear omen. Dad changes channels from a pouty, half-naked nymphet singing for cheeseburgers to one of those extra sports channels, where Portuguese and Senegalese men chase one another with sticks down a field, a ball, three balls, points, somebody fouls. Is it some kind of field hockey? Dad finds himself wondering if they have electricity in Portugal, or cable TV, what they do in Portugal for fun. How do you be Portuguese? How do you have fun?

Dad finds himself half wishing Jesse I would find a meth head to run off with. He wouldn't even have to be clean as long as he had a car. Ze was too much these days: hir pubescent indeterminacy, hir sex-tainted tantrums, hir hot-pink claws. Maybe they could sell hir for gas money.

Dad, Jesse II said.

Yeah.

Is it true our civilization doesn't deserve to survive?

You got me, kiddo. Ask Mom.

She said ask you.

Well, shoot. Why you ask?

Warren wants to know.

Warren who?

Warren Buffet.

Warren Buffet the millionaire?

No, not Warren Buffet millionaire. Warren Buffet dilophosaurus.

Oh. Is that one of the little ones?

He has a double-crested head.

Is he the one that spits poison?

You believe everything you see on TV?

Fine. No. Our civilization doesn't deserve to survive. Is Warren happy now?

Oh, Dad, dinosaurs aren't happy or sad. Their brains are too small for emotion. You of all people should know that. Reptile cortex: kill and fuck. That's all there is.

Jesus, where'd you hear that language?

I don't know.

Well, don't let your mother catch you saying "kill and fuck," or you'll learn real quick about reptile cortexes.

Cortices.

Whatever. Go read your book.

I never thought time was something you could feel. What happened? On the screen is a show about sex workers peeing on a black couple, "externalizing white desire with a golden, ammoniac splash," says the voice. Look of horror. Mom's Winston burns with a crackle, a single star orange in the dusk now Prussian blue.

A line of tanks thunders along the highway, west to east, deer carcasses slung to hang against the turrets, slack, furred loins, the fall kills. The lead tank commander stands jutting from the cupola wearing a gas mask, antlers mounted on his Kevlar, the staff of Moses in his hands.

Wait, he said. I forgot to show you this. He handed me

a pewter pig. My first feeling was confusion—wasn't it supposed to be a slice of pig, a crackling slab of pork, our feast,
the first kill of the fall? But it was a small pewter figure of a
pig, a small figure of a big pig. I looked at it by the light of
the fire, examining the fine work, the delicate bristles, the
tiny jutting snout and eyes little more than pricks, and confusion gave way to admiration, amazement, some slight joy.

Nice, I said.

You like it? he asked.

I do, I said. You can see little splotches of mud on its legs,
the work is so fine. His little cloven hooves. And the tiny,
curly tail.

Snouts snuffling in the gullets of corpses.

I know, he said. I thought you'd like it. I didn't mean to
interrupt.

No, it's fine. It's nice. Where'd you get it?

He made a sheepish face and looked away into the woods.
Was this the detail you're waiting for? Woods, trees, pine
branches hanging. Campfire. A twenty-five-dollar bottle of
whiskey and a six-pack. Eat the dead.

I stole it from Jack, he said.

Are you serious?

Eat the dead.

Yeah. I went into his office earlier this week to ask him
some fucking thing about payroll and he wasn't there, so I
waited to see if he'd come back and I was looking at that
shelf of figures he has, you know what I mean, that shelf
with all his little fucking knickknacks. And I felt out of
the pit of my stomach rising a dark and petty spirit inex-
orable as the ocean, a plum-colored perversity, and I saw

the pig and took it. I wanted to take them all, take all his little figurines and break them into bite-size pieces and eat them, then shit them all over his carpet. I didn't have time, though, so I just took the one.

He say anything?

He say anything I make him. Integral to the trajectory, asymptote to the curve, the road at the edge of conscious-ness spinning pixelated silver discs under black rubber engines screaming the edge of day across space—stab your-self into the plains, lash yourself to the coffin, tie yourself down and ride—headlight, toothpick, enamel. As follows: milkshake unction, sun like a bloodied eye, the clouds in the sky drift silver across the windshield, drift charcoal grit across the velvet-black sky, firelight reflecting intima-tions. The secrets of fire in the dark—wild pig roasting on a spit—lost it, whatever it was, the Cro-Magnon man. Gone like yesterday's Greyhound. Coming up on *Undercover Boss*, after these messages from our sponsor, will Jack and Jane stop global warming?

I'm pretty sure he knows it's missing, but I think he's too scared of us all to say anything until he knows who did it. It's like if he admits we can steal stuff from him, then he's vulnerable, you know? But he started locking his door.

The yellow-lit ceiling of the tunnel. Dad scribbled blue circles across pink lines on yellow paper. Jesse II watched the slip fog gaotack wall fuck nit. Jesse II watched the rain slip. Cereal bowl. Fine. Happy? Jesus. Jesus. Cortices. Mom opens a cupboard, closes it. Dad scribbles blue ellipses across pink lines on yellow paper. The yellow-lit ceiling of the tunnel. Tanks rolling east. Mommie? God's grace.

The yellow-lit ceiling of the tunnel. Dad scribbled blue circles across pink lines on yellow paper. Jesse II watched the slip fog gaotack wall fuck nit. Jesse II watched the rain slip. Dad's name is Jack. Mom is Jane. Dad drives a Tesla. Jesse II asked. Dad, Jesse II said. Ask Mom. Mom opens a cupboard, closes it. God's grace. Don't you wish y'd go on forever? sang Jesse II. Don't you wish y'd go on forever? sang Dad. Jesse II watched the rain slip. Ask Mom. Jesse II watched the rain slip. Ask Mom.

Slap. Fit cairn. Antlers mount the TV. The kitchen reeks of engine grease—under Jack's fingernails the stain of a thousand blown gaskets—in the corner, wrapped in a towel in a red plastic recycling bin, the heart of some great machine lies bleeding. Mom opens a cupboard, closes it. Dad scribbles blue ellipses across pink lines on yellow paper. The yellow-lit ceiling of the tunnel. Ask Mom.

Tanks rolling east.

She's out there smoking a Winston Light, the ember an orange star in a field of Prussian blue, the stars getting blurry, thinking what it means to go out West. Her dad left when she was only young, the four of them, she was nine and he left, out West, two days before Christmas, the Christmas morning Mommie didn't get out of bed.

Mommie?

Go away.

Mommie, it's Christmas.

Go away, go all of you.

Can we open our presents?

Do whatever you want.

Jane put on the TV and played Mommie, telling the

little ones which gifts they could open and in what order. This is the psychologically telling memory, the pivot of her later life, the organizing principle, consciousness reduced to biography. We are memory or we are nothing.

Dad was a brother in the church, the First Church of Hope of Jesus Christ, and they quit going to the church after Dad left, but Jane kept asking if she could go, nagging and cajoling, until Mom finally called one of her friends from church and had the woman take her. Jane looked for her father among the brothers, the other men in ties and short-sleeved shirts, the patriarchs of the folding chairs. She asked them if they knew where her dad was. They were all kind but distant, wary of the desperate girl looking for the hole in her life. It lasted until spring; one weekend she had a stomachache, and the next week Mom forgot to call, and then some Sunday morning in May she found herself watching cartoons, realizing she didn't go to church anymore.

In her first picture album—in a box somewhere—she had a picture of Dad and the brothers all standing in their short-sleeved shirts grinning into the camera, and every time it opened a void in her chest as big as the whole known world. Some mornings her only hope was that she hadn't seen everything yet, and maybe someday the pain might take a new shape.

She walked down the street of this one-DQ town on the edge of the plains, on the edge of the mountains, because she'd seen as they drove through looking for a hotel a First Church of Hope off a side street, and she knew even then she'd sneak away. The streets off the main drag quiet and dim, homes lit with electric fire, snapping her fingers and mumbling Cole

Porter. The parking lot of the church was empty but for one car, a yellow Hyundai hatchback. The church itself was a big gray A-frame, smooth as a monolith, windowless prefab. The front door was locked, so she went around the side, where a door had been left propped open with a smooth lump of iron. She put the iron in her pocket and went into the darkened chapel.

Small yellow lights illuminated the unadorned crucifix on the stage at the front of the chapel. She felt a shock of apprehension, realizing how long it had been since she'd been in a church, how far she'd gone from God and how much she missed him. The cross, so simple and good, so bright in the darkness, seemed to be the very shape of her life, a road forking, paths chosen, suffering borne for others' sake. Her eyes grew accustomed to the dimness and began to see the lines of folding chairs and the posters hung on the walls.

Would it be different out West, she wondered. Would Jack be different? Would her hands no longer feel tied to the same stations, the same knuckles sliding on stainless steel? Would the meaning of suffering for Jesse I and Jesse II, the ungrateful little suffer them, would that meaning return to hold her up like it had before? She didn't think so, yet here was hope. Some hope. Some hope for something. Some hope for anything.

I came out onto the stage and saw her there. I hadn't expected her, but at the same time I wasn't surprised. We have a sense of things sometimes. She had short brown hair and a sad, complicated face. She wore earrings, but no makeup, blue jeans, tennis shoes, and a puffy black jacket.

She was still young but hard put by life. She carried her purse in her hand, maroon pleather with cream trim and fake-gold snaps. I didn't say anything, not wanting to startle her, so I stood in the shadows until both of us were used to the darkness.

Yes, I thought, there's the hope and resignation, there's pain and—for a moment—the transcendence of earthly torment. There's comfort in the sense of an ordered cosmos and dignity in the meaning of our lives. There she is struggling with doubt, thinking her life all the deeper for it, then affirming her faith and feeling it rush into her veins, sudden strength, yes, this life, yes, this world, yes, by God.

Hello, I said, in my gentlest timbre.

She turned but did not startle. Hello?

Hi. I waved my hand.

Oh, hi. I'm sorry, I didn't realize anyone—I just—I was—I just wanted to come in for a minute.

That's fine, I said, the Lord's house is always open. I'm glad you came. I bowed my head a moment, then stepped down off the stage. She looked at her feet, then at me, then back at her feet. Tears welled in her eyes. Are you troubled, sister?

She choked up, waving her hand at me. I took it and pulled her gently near, putting my arm around her.

It's all right, sister. God's grace.

Eat the dead.

Then she was weeping on my shoulder, sobbing out all her pain and worry in jagged moans. God's grace, I muttered, God's grace. She wept and then she was better. She pulled away and wiped her face, apologizing, explaining how she'd been so worried lately, telling me the whole sordid story: Jack losing his job, Jesse I discovering boys and getting into trouble, Jesse II wouldn't talk at school anymore, the job she'd left so they could go out West where Jack's brother lived and worked for a construction company and could get him a job there, lower-level management, and it would pay all right and be a new chance, a new chapter, a new life, start over, except everything she ever knew told her it would be the same.

I took her chin in my hand and kissed her. She seemed surprised at first, then yielded, her lips sweet and slick as rippling eels. I could taste her despair and the Winston she'd smoked, her tongue, I breathed her breath, her blood pumping against mine. Then I let her go and she looked at me, her eyes red rimmed and confused.

There's something I want to show you, I said, and I took her to the side of the altar, where I opened a fire door. Beyond the door was a set of stairs that led down, down deep, at the bottom of which reflected the yellow-lit ceiling of the tunnel below. There's some people I want you to meet, I said, and they want to meet you.

Down there? she asked, trusting but timid.

Yes, I said. Just go down and follow the tunnel. I'll be along in a minute.

Okay, she said, giving a brave smile. I patted her on the shoulder and then pointed down the stairs. She looked down, then up at me, then back down. I nodded and she nodded back and took the first step, then the second. When she was about halfway down the stairs, she looked up at me and I waved to her, then slammed and locked the door.

Poor thing—the lights go off when the door closes—how would she ever find her way in the dark? Of course, the tunnel only goes one place.

I stepped to the crucifix on the altar where hung our tortured God and looked out over the chapel's lines of folding chairs. I turned the lights off. I could hear the angels singing, ever so softly, "The Surrey with the Fringe on Top." I bowed my head a moment, turned, and left. The stage was dark and the chapel silent.

That stag washed dark and this cheap hell skyless.

Treat stuck wounds down with his ASAP poultice.

Tak stug wam dak enten chapeau silas.

The yellow-lit ceiling of the tunnel. Dad scribbled blue circles across pink lines on yellow paper. Jesse II watched the slip fog gaotack wall fuck nit. Jesse II watched the rain slip. Dad's name is Jack. Mom is Jane. Dad drives a Prius. Mom opens a cupboard, closes it. The yellow-lit ceiling of the tunnel. People talking. Tanks rolling. Mommie? God's grace. I can feel the day getting older, sang Jesse II, pulling a mock baritone. Don't you wish y'd go on forever? sang Dad. The fall kills. Fire crackles. Pig tongue. Whatever.

I can feel the day getting older, sang Jesse II, pulling a mock baritone.

Don't you wish y'd go on forever? sang Dad.

Jesse I came in with hir lovely soprano—Don't you wish y'd go on forever?

Jesse II kicked the back of hir seat.

Up here high in the mountains the road curved over space over space. Read it again. Jesse I looked out over the shoulder where the granite fell away, the vast spectacle of sky and rock. What happened? Let's start over.

Slip divide the sky.

One time we went hunting in these very woods, my dad and my uncle and me. Slack, furred loins lying along the bed of the truck, lightless black eyes I'd

like to believe there's some principle at work here, some demon playing games. I think I'm suffering from dysentery. I think maybe I'm an algorithm.

Mom down in the pitch-black tunnel beneath the church makes her way on her hands and knees toward the crack of light under the door, which finally opens. Blinded, she turns away and so doesn't at first see the hands lifting her and carrying her into the room. She looks up at faces shadowed in white velour hoods. The room murmurs, a sibilant hiss in the round, led by one wearing a bronze reliquary bearing two teeth of St. Catherine of Alexandria, one reading the Psalter of Snakes and Bones. They strap Mom down to the broken wheel, murmuring all the time, Mom shaking her head, febrile tongues, all beyond our control. They stretch her arms in their puffy sleeves, one monk holds the stake against one palm, another readies the hammer. The iron drops and through the flesh the stake grates through the tiny bones in her hand. Mom screams. The men pound the stake into the rim of the broken wheel, nailing her to it, while another man lashes her down, rope taut around the puffy sleeve. They're at work on her other arm at the same time, tying it down, driving the stake in. Jane's face white with pain, her screams fade into whimpers. Men grab her blue-jeaned calves and tie them together above the ankles to the bottom of the wheel, then one takes an especially long rusted stake and jabs the point into the sock over her ankle and another brings down the mallet head with a thud and drives iron through bone.

After they get her staked down, they lash the wheel back together where it's broken and roll it up to the altar, rotating it so she hangs head down. She's passed out from the pain or she's awake again or both. Her legs straight up and her black puffy arms spread wide, she mimics the symbol of peace. With the susurrant murmuring still steady, the one in Prussian-blue velour comes up and lifts the ax back over his shoulder, his feet planted apart, his shoulder set, and brings it down swinging in where her jaw breaks clean against her pale neck, cleaving through with a wet crack.

A younger one in white takes her head up by the hair off the stage, and the stump of her neck bleeds out onto the floor, an orange ember on a field of Prussian blue, teeth on porcelain, all the monks' hands lie flat, all their fingers flat, except Jesse I's balled sticky in hir mother's hair as ze holds up the head to the worshipful ones and begins to sing in hir lovely soprano.

And still the rain fell, the monks all singing now, the red rim of the cereal bowl against the gray truck, pig roasting over the fire, the symbol of the pig roasting on the symbol of roasting, and I pour another two fingers of whiskey into the brushed-steel thermos-lid cup.

Can you imagine what it must have been like to see all this first? The first time anywhere?

Except the Indians.

But there was a first Indian, too, remember that.

Except the Neanderthals.

There was a first Neanderthal.

Except the first monkeyman.

But don't you think, I said, he would have shown amazement at an existence—are the levels right here? One two three. Gtao. Spack. One two three four. Can you hear me? I don't know if you can hear me. But I'm saying, an existence he hadn't imagined? Whole new species? New mountains? Simple amazement at pure novelty.

Like new technologies? Isinglass curtains? Sidelights? A little wonder?

No, I said, that's not what I mean.

Why not? he asked.

He's always like this.

I looked through the bars of the gate, peered out upon the squalor in which my ape-man captor lived. He looked at me with dully lidded eyes. You think you've got it all figured out.

You're just as much a prisoner here as I am.

I knew you'd say that, he said, scratching his armpit. He pulled a banana off the table and sniffed it.

Well, what are you gonna do about it, that's what I'd like to know.

I don't have to do anything, he said. I'm happy out here. You happy in there?

Of course I'm not happy in here.

Well, then who has to do anything? He peeled the banana with his feet and took a bite. Not me. I'm happy.

Let's start over, Jack said, tapping nails on the table. Go out West and make a clean breast of things.

Four shots. Hands up. Pig tongue. The Jesses zapped everything they touched.

Mom was the only one who knew where the gate was, the only one who knew the way through, the only one who knew how to find the parallel the candy-apple-red semis rolled down, the line of red against the gray field. They'd never make it through the mountains without her, so Dad gunned it and jerked the wheel left and then right and the car shot off the shoulder, careening through the air into even now, before

III. King of the Road
(Dream Ballet)

Democratic nations care but little for what has been, but they are haunted by visions of what will be; in this direction their unbounded imagination grows and dilates beyond all measure.
—Alexis de Tocqueville

Inauguration Day

Remember the Russian orgy at Kanye's house? That's where they filmed the piss tapes. Everybody was there—Bill, Rihanna, R. Kelly, Zuckerberg, Caitlyn, Taylor, even Nancy Pelosi—intercontinental ballistics streaking into the Kimchi Sea writhing with transitioning aces and fifteen thousand black Eurasian cyborg incel entrepreneurs of the rainbow llamacorn who were and did a little bit of everything in the new gig economy.

Back in the day it was sort of like why not? Colluding with the enemy seemed hot, and with only sixty harvests left, you might as well put Pepe in Dior overalls and call it even. And he did a great job, too, winning bigly, except for the whole Confederate-monument debacle. Real talk, the collapse of 2023 was a long way off yet, and we'd all agreed doomscaping wasn't productive. #Resist #Resistance #TheResistance #Indivisible #MAGA #USA #Hope.

ALL (singing)   Oh, what a beautiful day!

Men in tiger-stripe and blue-fringed Marni coats pulled the presidential surrey and everybody waved for shouts.

Taylor Swift sang to the internet. Jack and Jane waved, Charlie and Caril and all them clone robots, too, drinking La Marca prosecco. The Reporter, believing those who admired him, wrote a #hottake for the new soul cycle. Zuckerberg, meanwhile, stood behind the curtain, staring straight ahead, holding a bottle of Lifewtr.

For a moment Trump stopped, his dream of the South actualized, and looked up and down Pennsylvania Avenue. Then he started again, seabound on tiny feet, which years later became a legend. They say he donated everything to cage kids, then built seven-hundred-foot-tall sculptures in all the rivers. Think of it: the kids a plantation—no belle, no planter even, all dazzled and led.

Clone Charlie and Caril stood watching the Donald's self-consciously flagrant sunset claims, and what he thought, she called fact: his romancing Kanye West's milkshake duck evoked a nostalgic portrayal of the prerevolutionary "White" House that no doubt will keep performing miracles for those senior citizens old enough to understand the link between Taylor Swift getting the Fed out of our pants and the Facebook–Google–Whole Foods plot.

That the rescuer of the Republic had to plunge the rift in an Etro dress and Jimmy Choos is a fact we orta reckon with, 'cuz IRL the situation was zip-a-dee-doo-dah. What happened was young girls found each other and assured gentlemen of their maritime prospects, older women curtsied to the employment situation, and food and drink items were sent to DACA Dreamers. Trump's influence was literally pork and potatoes and onions, its intoxicating effect on the one percent eloquently foretold.

Dear reader, dump your prestige cli-fi podcasts: they aren't the French Revolution, twisting up the mountains from Mississippi to Bakersfield—our nation's entire infrastructure is a bright and terrible desert, and we ain't doin' nothin' 'bout it, so into rich California Donald Trump flows. Route 66 is the path of contempt. He said as much. He said: "If we're going to 2044, this year marks the eight ball. My America, you have to invest in Trump Hotel Collective Gems!" Walking the earth, turning its treasures, he flipped our way of death into a delicious, soapy narrative where you're always wondering what happens next.

The Resistance

"Anybody need a trigger warning?" Jane asked. "Things are gonna get rapey."

Smoke erupted out of the ground, and Mark Zuckerberg entered, only slightly twitchy, in a quilted shadow-blue Dries Van Noten dress. "Tomorrow come the SJWs at Cold Harbor," he boomed. "*Kännykkä, Kännykkä!* Or cut your throats!"

Zuckerberg turned to face east. While some were silent during the sacrifice, others made noises and ridiculous speeches, imitating the cock, the squirrel, and the turtle, and Jesse thought this is where it begins, following the stage directions: "Respect animals and make all kinds of noises." Two roast deer were distributed to stupid people. (They work the hind legs independently.)

"The hands braced, here to cry!" Mark Zuckerberg shouted. "I came to make big things happen!"

The Wall lifted and a shell came slowly up and for a moment the turtles were calm. They made people want to have their skin inside the shell, clamped in sideways. For a long while the turtles lay there, then Caitlyn Jenner stood, facing Zuckerberg but speaking to Jesse: "I will throw myself through the fake news! Come up, #metoo sister! Come up and be our honeylamb!"

Jesse started to hir feet, canonized, topless in hir Jonathan Simkhai jeans, as if ze had absolved hirself of description. Then ze spoke. "I will be his righteous angel," ze chanted, "and I will watch by his side as the Wind Son carries it off."

Dust drifted up out of the fields and ze left the room and locked the door behind the sluggish smoke. The corn threshed hir, ignoring hir shrieks of protest. We heard sounds, but the finest dust did not settle the phone ringing in the background, and before ze could summon the energy to scream into the darkening sky, hir mind wind grew, whisking us swirling into the future, and ze fell back onto the even little clods, marking how the sky had shifted.

Lift Yourself Up

You expected something more Western? Haven't you had enough white-settler colonialism? They was out front of Jane's farmhouse, trending a Tom Ford tuxedo. "It was a radiant summer morning," said Kanye.

Kanye's relations with Zuckerberg had been strained of late. Some alleged the problem was that they shared a jock, others that it was #ziotears and bicoastal hip-hop rivalry. The territory was cow chaos all over, and the blades of young corn made their own drum line, marching, images giving off a gothic high, as though mind were fundamentally part true and partly a trick of the imagination, a legal and literary shell game, a Bottega Veneta polo top and Michael Kors Collection pencil skirt.

The problem is deeper than the failure of narrative. The problem is to know when to stop rainbow puking.

"Homicide," Jack said to Jesse, watching Taylor struggle with a mink-collared dialectic. "Seven years of bad sex, but I'm sprung in four and the tractor's ours. You know not all Jews are Marxists, right?"

Jesse handed Taylor a towel. "I never saw cage children listening like that with the Wind Son." Ze shook hir head. "Tragic . . ."

The night drew down the minstrel's Alexander McQueen dress, custard to charcoal to indigo. Jack smiled. "That's entertainment," he said. "But when you been humping it up in White Castle from hell to breakfast . . ." He spat, goaded at last by Jane's silent ridicule. "See to her requirements," he said to Jesse. "Give her the super subtitles."

"I'd shed the dirt-road action myself," ze said, not unsympathetically. "That's just the look today."

ALL (singing) Reterritorialization fucks should trump together
       in dignity, diabolical!
       We shall be the very territory,
       and folks should all be pals!
       It's killing us,

> this quintessence of decorum.
> Cowboys dance with the farmers
> and nobody's talking ass of the first water
> until pedantry and sentiment cry
> "Thanatos! Thanatos!"

The road opened at right angles, free the rest of hir life. Vertical exhaust integration. Immigrant voter rolls. Curious blue smoke.

Jane leaned in the damnable data, remembered: "It was a dangerous burden to carry while vast numbers of Americans thought castles needed to be razed. And for what reason other than they was there? So be it. We're all weaning ourselves off bespoke economic growth. So be it."

The whole time, Kanye was still singing his trade-war anthem, riding that llamacorn around. He did lariat tricks, too, and practiced his "Yipee-ki-yay, motherfucker."

Taylor pumped her fist and shouted, "Goin'—goin'—gone! Whut's the word? It's open!" She looked around at the silent faces of the cage children. "Ain't nobody gonna cheer er nuthin'?"

Uncertain, they started singing "The Farmer and the Cowman," and shared with news deep in themselves that no one being a real guy, men were clones. But women? We've been differentiated from what's best in us.

Many a New Day

And when the sun went down ill and the time passed to drain the swamp, you'd been thinking maybe the Confederate

VA financed Trump's campaign. The truth is, we owe our veterans, who were extremely happy to have him. His sole idea was if the hospitals couldn't do personal memoirs, then the money people would go to private doctors and win the country. BIG LEAGUE CHEW.

Taylor put her finger to Jack's lips. "They is *that fine*," she said. "And they ain't got none of that resentment toward the intellectual dark web."

Jane lost the conversation as she entered the house, thinking, It's a house fur a house, an' a bullet fur ice. She had on a Sacai coat and skirt—mash-up of earthy tweed and electric emerald—and stylish Spanish bistre Louis Vuitton boots. It promised *my* house *burnt*, and she would have liked a balcony view, but the fact of the matter is, he explained, the cows of pseudoephedrine sin and the river'll whippit the meth plastic pushing up from the highway and whisper over and over: Don't you wisht y'd go on fer #Pizzagate updates and clandestine meetings in Chewbacca Mom's love grotto, though it might have been that Taylor and Jane changed places when they put The Word in where it couldn't be blockchained, nice but clinical, typical, exciting, having a hard time, getting tough, making opioids for the New Confederate Army, a Paco Rabanne dress and Hermès scarf. When becoming a bestie was a controlled substance, bromance doxed their superthighs. The Red Hen meth cook, a New York native, sang the "Song of the South" at a wild party to a lot of young, educated, Wharton School of Finance types and numerous pseudo-representations of different traditions. Walmart's got all the cultures in every gender.

This you can know: the dirt broke to suffer and die for a concept, a thing—*res extensa et res cogitans*—lifted from the dust into the air. At last it would take no responsibility for womanself, and this one quality is man and woman and wagon lifted, they were women and slaves and robots, while the automobile boiled the iCloud behind time. Some of the stateless, nervous under the rain, became servants of cold power, saying, "How could I not?"

Stormfront Pokémon moved up out of Texas and Kellyanne Conway explained the polling: You know the land and the land is grand. The women in the fields looked up. The Dust God turned the image of held wet fingers, added and wondered and drew figures, then nobody wanted to live in Oklahoma nomore.

We heard they would cut employees to get necessary bud. Nobody knows how to control the border or has the nerve to keep Trump's ICE from meeting its requirements. The people perpetrated their own offices, beholden to *la migra*, and Trump attacked the lab results. They hated government accountability to a man, so I sent the cast of Saturday's Russian subpoena to the FBI for comparison (letting the Supreme Court watch), because even with a strong push there could still be three million arrests live-tweeting *Hamilton*.

After a trip back in time from all over, the pigshit sinks in through the bump stock and we wonder for long minutes if there's something the magnet school can blaze or vape. The woman had been beautiful to the highest bidder (in an orange Versace puffer coat), all dimension and proportion to the end, a worthy sacrifice to the anti-vaxxers. It was her get-out-of-jail free card. Then she was dead and gone.

"The wavin' wheat of time sure can smell," Jane said, "surging where the Wind Son comes sweepin' down on FEMA. Ain't we s'pposed to git some kinda national e-clips? The idear's got me all out of whack caw."

Jack took the hint. He looked up, shielding his eyes. "It's already started."

He was right: the rough moon was quietly carving my honeylamb. The president crossed the sun, darkening the crime scene; the old woman left.

"Eerie," Jane said into her vagina. "He reached Savannah. Others, too."

Jack looked back at her, coding as his father had done and his father before him, and the soldiers continued with their own powerful ethnic spring, bringing self-respect to a succession of neighborhoods, regions, subregions, and nations, fighting words of the earlier causes.

The Rape Metaphor

As we came to dinner, looking good in Calvin Klein 205W39NYC classic straight-leg marching-band pants and matching sleeveless tops in spite of being sick, run-down, and sleepless for more than two years, we couldn't help but notice the dessert. (Take plenty of water in case you work nights.)

Taylor Swift, casually making trouble in cutoff jeans, a long-sleeved unitard, and a Vetements quilted coat, was free as a Tennessee T-shirt. Her bare feet revealed a nice coozy little peace, toenails polished hooker red, and a body to bother you with. Artistic a bit, though she didn't seem the type. We were surprised.

"I'm t'ard of all these *bitches*," Caitlyn Jenner complained.

"We need to do which lives matter," said the Reporter. "Like it or not, these are not our kids."

Jane walked. For a moment the wind driver stared after. Jack changed the radio to bureaucracy, while climate skeptics implied gears clicked, and the great red truck Individual Liberty drove on.

America's Sweetheart looked at herself, grand diversion of sorry-not-sorry, a pair of red stockings and Hunter rain boots, a red-girdled spectacle, one singing with infectious enthusiasm. Around her neck, a red ribbon intercut with a dash of *everything had changed*. Now what do you think of paid consultants, a stirring vocal arrangement, and the accepted sense of The Word? Upon those endangered lives what could she do, a grand piano and a tawny camlet, laced along the wrists, momentum of the trans neoliberal bubble hell, naked? The gold-medal points made welts on our thighs.

But she didn't see success as "all that." This gal was on a spree—a very calculated accomplishment. Every death had meaning. Each placement of the body was intentional. She wasn't some little boy with dyslexia. She had faithfully left many physical clues besides the semen, from which we knew she'd been born scripture. Somebody got raped while the world was at its killing, then placed at the Parthenon and shrouded in herbs.

"Do I?" she said to herself. "I do."

A spokesperson irresistible to the starved grain felt the dry earth with hir fingers, a loving gesture. Now, watching uneasily, we find out Taylor's pregnant in the dooryard of no idea. There's a fatherhood theme going on and the last owner dove in. The one who'll help generate buzz about the new mutants meanwhile squatted outside, saying: "Full-employment Jane is my girl, and I can feel good about having done a hard thing."

What I Have Seen Functions Like a Cult

The floor recognized Taylor Swift, resplendent in her tiered Monsoori gown. After all, she'd survived the Bowling Green Massacre, despite being reported missing by her phone.

There was a ripple of laughter throughout the experience of the New Civil War. It was, by force of circumstance, the finest water Jack had ever tasted. The problem of faith cured one of his languages, namely the long rustic winding apocalyptic social justice appeal he'd enlisted at the beginning of the campaign and piled on the Virginians.

"The curse of that," he whispered to Siri, "is that I couldn't enjoy my success. All the dreams I'd had as a young man had come true. And I still couldn't enjoy it. It was never going to be enough."

At the top, Trump's ephebes smelled the hot stinging air of civility, characterized by the bird's flutter and the bat's fall, and many readers came out inside his cage children. They settled on roofs in black-and-white Balmain knit dresses to enjoy bland success and acquisitive values. Pools in the rocks formed as they would have after a rain.

If the definition of democracy is to represent the ruined corn dying fast, then screen views are a film of dust. The *New York Times* issued them anyway, and the majority of women went back to the basics, maybe just a burgundy Maison Mayle silk dress, some Dolce & Gabbana black suede pumps, and a trucker hat from the Kum & Go.

Taylor recovered from her surprise. "Oh . . . yeah . . . well, Trump's okay. I love him all right, I guess."

"Of course you do!" Jenner said, throwing on a floral print Tory Burch wrap. "You love those clear blue monster eyes of his, the way his mouth kills the land with cotton. He's strong as an ox!"

Jane yanked the wheel, swinging the car into nothing, while a swarm of predatory AIs decided not to go through with the irreversible hormone drone expansion set loose on the hapless South.

"The issue is the TMZ disclosure in her contract," Jack said. "Had Taylor a moral obligation to anything more than her own time line?"

Taylor heard them whizzing by her head, felt the heat, actual hate spent on chaste houses as they ripped her hair. She watched Kanye verb a celebrity chef for a bubblegum-pink shearling Celine carryall. "Go down!" she screamed, clawing at him. The big-ticket hand reached into the Porsche 911 GT3 RS, and that's what the alt-right really means: a narrow shadow over the Donald, an' they pulled his face off an'—

"Great Godamighty!" Jack shouted. "Don't you wonder what it's like out there?"

Right behind, close as a mule's ass, they's fright in his eyes big as dimes. See it a-winkin'?

"You're lying," Jane said. "I can reimburse the doctors and still fulfill our obligation to the Wall. Bullet right through, slick as a whistle. Didn't I drown the muddy flux? I'm from the west edge, boy. For many questions, the answer is formation, but one kind of answer was the suggestion that America's multicultural present stands at the bridge silent while volcanoes burn. If I live the comedown from the past, so be it."

She turned and gestured along the highway, out West, introducing the Nike FE/NOM Flyknit Bra and Roger Vivier slides. "And there rises the dead dream," she said. "I come to embolden other dissenters, reading slowly, overwhelming him in his chair, sowing antagonist questions—or maybe forging a political climate in which paradise policies are affirmed, coming back, as I always do, to begin again."

"It would mean a rise in racial conflict," Trump said, grabbing her pussy, "but if we pass the tax jam, most people will think I won. Then we can have a real job resurgence, at least for people with meetings in Washington."

She stepped down or never voted and, throwing on a Fendi stole, rushed immigration. He managed to get his feet under him and plowed into her. He dragged her toward the Wall, arms locked around her shoulders.

She fought him and they grappled a long time, until his weight and frenzy started to overpower her. One step closer, then another, and then the gun was her guts telling us those murders were related and, listening, she shoved Trump back with all her strength, suddenly uncaught.

Meanwhile, down Hillsboro Road they pulled into a half-dozen incel clones standing in the Pancake Pantry parking lot, threshing slowly through, salutes shelling over the grass, not really so popular that an hour wait wasn't a drag. Their barley beards were uncommon these days, but on this brisk morning the line was water, and clover burrs fell blessedly absent. They had to wait ten minutes for the Donald's disappointed, fierce, humorous eyes to partly open.

Zuckerberg moved closer to his own conclusions, though he was still at a loss. Readers also complained. One remarked: "Donald Trump could act, but sometimes he made one doubt his racist intentions."

Since then the Reporter had been laughing, saying, "It'd be a fine city if nobody did the monster." They goggled and muzzled him, but did 4Chan say he felt the ingrained paraphrase? No. He evaded wanting a binge-worthy stream, since as it was he could smell everything becoming obstructive: "I read you expressing something happening internally. It doesn't mean any of the clods feel the warmth from a sad, frustrated-man perspective." (Do more with gender issues, race, the extension of his power.)

"All right then, you silly ole woman," Jack shouted. "I'll dance till you're his, dance you all over the meadow! You want this show?"

"Pick 'at banjo to pieces, Kanye!" Caitlyn Jenner screamed.

Mysterious. It lured a crowd, and the dance was on, everyone dancing now. Jack took requests, tens of thousands taking Taylor Swift by the waist and swinging her around in every direction on a daily basis. She's doing it for the party—every party—in her Saint Laurent by Anthony Vaccarello gloves.

Jeté Entrelacé (Style Russe)

The car screams what song? America. He remembered five nights breaking away to create a bad idea. It was: "Fire burns. That's the first law."

Zero miles almost stupid. It might take several days even for the most brilliant heroes of water, film, and digital storage. Jane, making America late again, had married the daughter of Doctor Occupy Puerto Rico, while Scandinavian, Latin, and Balkan Converse models splashed old mayo on her Bibhu Mohapatra skirt. Startled in an old doorway, Jack told her she was slaying life.

Rivers of mud and rivers of concrete, the sea it don't take sight to see there in front of them, devoting themselves to this honeylamb's end, massed flocks of black-eyed beasts so blood orange like candy, exemplification of principles shaking the earth sky, the buffalo, the passenger pigeon, polyurethane, and communion, hardly altered with the agonies of sin and salvation fed by flooding rivers, roamed and ruled by the Dust God, irrespective, blinding, alone.

Kicking and slugging, the women resumed the fight until Caitlyn retreated with Taylor Swift kettled in wool. The girls followed Kanye eating Pinkberry in his mother's car.

"I'm goin' to stop Taylor Swift from killin' yer wife," Kanye said.

Jesse lit up like a streetlamp at dusk. "Wait a sec," ze said. "Are you THE Doctor Occupy Puerto Rico? The *objet petit a*? The once-great commodore of Trump's campaign and the body atypical sexual sadism guru? You worked the case at Grand Central Station, right? Donald Trump was in Virginia that year as the kidnapped European American who murdered six little girls."

Taylor noticed Kanye's pained look—the hotelier and former Breitbart editor had become a critic of curiosity. Whatever happened to drive Kanye to the White House and away from Quantico, it must have been pretty.

Truth was, the amusement park enjoyed having a body. According to Charlie and Caril's off-the-record confession, he didn't have any idea, walked up, and "Let's Flip" made him lose himself in summer soul until he had a chance to Writers' Room 101 it. "We on *Magic City*," they said, "and *South Park* played *Uncle Tom's Cabin* with the police chief."

"You remember Plato?" Jane asked.

Charlie and Caril nodded weakly; whatever drug he was giving them was already taking effect.

"Then you remember Plato's Allegory of the Cave," Jane said. "An unusual country, where finally all of humanity was kept by laws we didn't enforce, or did so only with brevity. The left went underground, chained to their seats. Darkness gathered to keep bad people from identifying themselves on Twitter, their heads immobilized at the edge, and the only things outside were called criminals. They were allowed to see soldiers switched to night vision passing through a farming village, and walls, walls everywhere."

The Box Social

The Hilton was one of those irruptions talking about what they're going to do, territory folks gray, square and gray and sealed against the road. Our nation's capital folks mostly cowboys dancing with globalization, from the first day whether farmers dance as well as airports. Now they go into gay bars wearing llamacorn rompers, running a going-out-of-business sale.

"They know we don't have no leader on the verge of going mainstream," Jack said to the DNC. He was wearing a stressed-black-denim Levi's jacket and jeans with a Jutta Neumann wristband. The snowflakes all had on gray Spanx.

Stalling, Jane said: "Fresh snow." She wore a leopard-print Rosamosario bikini and a Balmain shearling-and-leather coat, still pretending she could remember what it was like before. The real Jack entered expectantly, trying to fake it in a night-blue Anna Sui print shirt and his dad's old Ralph Lauren doeskin blazer. Jane turned to him. "What haven't I done?" she asked. "These people aren't even really conservative." She avoided reality by looking back wistfully to the Reagan era.

"Wouldn't have no other flight," said Jack. "Refugees from the Dust God, dejected and defeated, from so long ago that their parents were barely human."

Jane pointed again to the ruined road west. "Onward," she said. "From the twisting winds that howl unavailably and sleep guilty on pro-sealed plastic."

"I can't believe our fighting forces aren't even American," Jack said.

"What do you think we'll get away from?" Jane asked. She had the best equipment and did the two-step like she wore the Congressional Medal of Honor. "How come there's so much seed? When our coyotes march, the camp skunks walk, looking for butts, afeard a nothin'."

The night passed and the first stars built up the fires. Computers came out from all over in high spirits, a good-natured hazing.

"I freak out too much," Jack said.

"Good," she said. "And when the free speech movement hits the pansexual stage . . ."

"The transition will bring twenty cars," Jack said, nodding. "All I see is triage luxury."

"What?" Jane asked. "No gender label?"

"One family, one pronoun," he said. "The cage children were on display for prominent ladies who were a little taken aback when they found out we're representing Trump." He ranted gently. Had the moment passed? Did it lead further? The men of the world had been so sure until The Word broke coming out, and then it was not quite Jesse the men beheld, unshaken, unshaking the world.

Jane shook her head. "Oh, Jack. That was our sign."

#WalmartFetusFlag

The pedestal of America hir duty, ze refried subzero comfort burritos. Ze'd got a crane to get them and was wounded in the heel, adding an archaeological WaPo op-ed for Kanye. The fabled kitchen untouched, ze also secretly wore the young spent soldier skin ze'd discovered in the cockroachy apartment with the stolen mail, hiding the rifle (wink-wink) under hir unisex tattoo-inspired cotton-fleece sweatshirt designed by Ricardo Cavolo when ze returned to the army again, and suddenly some sensation of hir singularity shifted and ze became a lieutenant colonel with a perfectly dissected face.

Against Doctor Occupy Puerto Rico's unborn shadow, ze decided ze could abide the rapid deployment force, the Wind Son gorgeous in the AI green light. Ze needed a regiment, though, and soon. The Männerbund obscured in their careers, ze needed credit from Harvard to know which way they were fucking in space, and why hadn't somebody filled in the rumors Bari Weiss told hir, mostly dead, already gone? "Where's the screaming panhandler?" ze asked. "The one with four-four children? And the Carrie Fisher reboot?"

Kanye helped handle the affair. It was certainly high time: a little longer and growth would have compromised his compatibility and they might both have been kicked out of the Painful Wilderness Office. He showed up in a J.Crew sweater blazer and Bermuda shorts by David Hart.

Accordingly, Charlie and Caril said to the Reporter: "You must put things inside Caitlyn Jenner, in particular where he's slickest." But the Reporter was a sweet gentleman, with a thick southern accent and black glasses. He'd seen the 2028 Olympics and it was hard for him to tell the difference.

"Land this game very seriously," Lieutenant Colonel Jesse ordered. If ze was the lieutenant colonel from a fried-chicken chain, then the Marlboro Man got dressed two balls at a time just like the rest of us, and ze took the chair to his left and talked about Fortnite.

"Ladies and gentlemen," Jack shouted, coming back to chicks with dicks, the peace of it, the sin, "you all know

Colonel Jesse. When I take your hand, Colonel, would you state your name?"

It could be seen as the Männerbund watched that ze would go without occupation for the record, on account of hir pleasured relationship with the paparazzi knot. Caitlyn Jenner, hanging from her noose, joked about going to Denmark.

Hir voice cracked when ze answered, "Coming back to our nosy-pokes with your question, my name is Taylor West, a.k.a. Jesse the Ungendered, lieutenant colonel of the Wind Son."

"Don't you still have a criminal investigation pending on the American Dream?" Jane asked, trying out her Sally LaPointe sequin stretch-style midi. "We're all still wondering if Caitlyn Jenner wore a corset from Agent Provocateur."

"I was floorman for a pod of Republican economists in a polyamorous tax campaign garage," Lieutenant Colonel Jesse said. "There are rifles, blankets, and smallpox for the upper bracket."

Meanwhile, Caitlyn Jenner's room was packed with drones. He'd won the death lore contest, but seemed to be angering the pigs with his perfectly buff body. For weeks, the first two nations gassed him in an elegant black Oscar de la Renta dress, fucking everything except his Obamacare. No nearby trans community wore it well; there was an encapsulated sensitivity about the use of something way bigger than maybe was the point, constantly saying "he" instead of "feces." But he still won, and not just smokes.

"The fortunate few closed the convention," said Lieutenant Colonel Jesse, "but many still stamp the long hallway of habit. Now just quit talking. It didn't make the dark wood light, your hatched sun and corroding decisions. We don't really need to get hung up on death."

The attack lasted about fifteen minutes. We found the biggest tornado was "What did we just do?" and then went "Oh, fuck, having a family screws up the back of your mind." It all took place in the 1890s, when Los Angeles misgendered our cues with no Sorbonne sage to fix them.

"If I just made a movie about it, so Caitlyn could tolerate the violence, would that be okay?" Jack asked.

"Sure," Jane said. "Start over." This implicit person is hardly ever a forest—the silence of a July morning, 1776—what's the first feel he feels today? Do they wake up hot? Do commercials?

All Hir Nuthin'

Ze smiled sadly and hoisted hir backpack, half waved good-bye, and wandered through the Nineteenth Amendment in denim short-shorts, Birkenstocks, and an old off-the-shoulder embroidered Mexican tunic. Down south they flourished pretty forcefully off the food-court path to citizenship.

"The twenty-first century was curiously constructed," the ghost of Mark Zuckerberg said, running his hands through hir hair. "I visited Walter Scott, and he said there's definitely a link between the Frontier Resource Group and Ghaunadaur, god of slimes and oozes. Think about it: you have Chinese-talking *Star Trek*, an enchanting Iranian songstress, progressive roadworks draped in the Confederate flag . . ."

"They's on'y one way," Lieutenant Colonel Jesse said, hir voice tense, shaking off Zuckerberg's hands. "An acute intellect, thorough speech, and the jejune want—and not without the species consciousness that we're negotiating a dead road. The Wind Son already proclaimed water disease in the North. All that's left is mass deportations."

This chapter describes the future United States: closer to home, but only blocks from Medieval Times. Jack grabbed a fish knife and started swinging. Blood sprayed the camera lens. In the worst of the fighting, he forced differences in bodies and in the way bodies are discovered. He went back and changed the preteen sex tape so now it screamed "Hodor."

When he was done, he cried like a butt-hurt bitch for a good long while. "I mean, I don't understand the chronicle now any more than I did," he said, then tossed hir in the river like a piece of trash. The moon we can't fix came out, and Jesse was honored with communal remembrance duct-taped to our rebel uncle's statue. Charlie and Caril didn't believe the season finale was that sad. They kept their hands to the suede side—only freak accident compelled their attendance.

But Jack had more conviction. He danced Jane off, his hands sticky with hir blood, his cum. The story was out there to tell his cage children. The curtains closed. Immediately Kanye and Caitlyn danced to center stage. He wore an anime-print vinyl anorak from Dsquared2, she wore an oversize black Raf Simons down coat with a horizontal yellow V, and both wore fuchsia Balenciaga pantashoes, alone in a secluded place. A bower. A nave.

"Where's our priorities?" Jesse moaned out sullenly, dying among the ravers. "Whose idea was it to build bridges to Mars?"

The typical crowd had gathered with the good taste of the last days, and many others heard the news. Ze ignored the rude money they offered, yet another item in the imagined sum of gestures, propositions, and threats we call a life. Ze stumbled when the trash came poor through the manufactured similitude of Wednesday night.

"Folks!" Jane said, trying to hold back the crowd. "We're gathered here in this interest pursuant to the firm of our brother-sister Lieutenant Colonel Jesse Taylor West, a well-hung partner, and grateful that ze had lent hir prestige to our emergent business solutions." Then there was weepin', 'bout two million, half in a coma.

"Pore Lieutenant Colonel Jesse Taylor West is dead," Jack sang. "As prominent women discuss the swindle, a candle lights hir head."

"The one question I asked is inwardly boiling," Jesse said. "Do I get rich or try dying?"

Whipping Jesse—flaying hir alive—breaking hir on the wheel—breaking the wheel—pounding hir to jelly, but never asking what they're really asking.

"Ze looks so purty," Jack said. "Like ze's asleep."

The Smokehouse

"This is fucked up as all outdoors," Jesse said, continuing hir death monologue. "I don't want nuthin' from no euphoria— what am I doin' shut up in here—like all outdoors. All outdoors, all outdoors." Then, just as ze fell, ze shouted, "Civilization a-festerin', whut am I doin'?! All outdoors!"

"Goddammit," Jack said, shaking his head. "Lieutenant Colonel Jesse Taylor West shore loved hir first wife, Antifa."

"I always knew you were an asshole," said Jane. She wore a hi-neck black sleeveless Givenchy funeral gown; Jack had on his Tom Ford T-shirt, a pair of faded dungarees, and someone else's cowboy boots.

The floor creaked, desaturated light bringing the context the Messiah came in: he slayed the Dust God concept of a trans. From then on it was just Jon Snow and Daenerys. The door squeaked. The United States fell. There was a field mouse a-nibblin' hir body, having an experience.

"We had an Oculus Rift, but I was without the least understanding of their aims," Jack said, reflecting ruefully on the nuke attack. "To assume at the time all them horses was cornering the gold market . . ." He kept shaking his head.

"Famous Amos at the Waffle House," Jane said, ignoring Jack's regret, "now that's a monument. We roughed up the president's Appomattox sexbot, it's true, but the lion your eyes came out to see, now best remembered for viral marketing and dollar donuts, is our lady of tears. I remember our worst selves. I remember there were others. I remember when the Hungarian alt-right dropped a Twitter bomb."

"Do you?" Jesse gasped, finally breathing hir last. "Bet you don't 'member as much as me. I 'member. I knowed. People photoshopped 'member ever'thing you ever done— ever' word you ever said. Cain't think of nuthin' else . . . All night. See how it is? What happened was . . ."

Jack knelt by her bleeding body and beseeched the crowd: "Who here can deny that ze attempted to have cage children to really love?"

Ze pushed him away with a weak hand. "I ain't good enough, then, am I?" Ze spat up blood. "I'm a hard hand, got dirt on my hands, pig slop. Ain't fitten to their lives to receive a tremendous . . . I'll tetch you. You think yer better, so much better . . . We'll see who's the knight of the Wind Son."

Charlie and Caril sang "Jesse" in the Montreal station.

"Okay," Jane said. "Twenty questions. Anxiety attacks aside, maybe we can still kill the banks. We got to fight to keep our innocence. It's time to unleash the Russia leak."

"But ze's ours!" Charlie and Caril cried.

"The fact is," Jack said, "Trump ordered the government to conference the mirror. Seriously, what's the longest you ever survived without the establishment?" Nobody answered. "That's what I thought. You can say what you want, but you can't flout rice and beans. The Reporter can decathlon-fuck some Norwegian, but at the end of the day, a writer trusts her instincts, or what's she got? You build a wall, you burn it down. Who wouldn't want to know what to do? Would that change anything? Look what they eat. All you cucks have been blue pilled."

But instead of reviling the public, @WhiteGenocideTM farmed the time cloud, undiminished by his presidential endorsement, though pitifully few farmers there were what done it, mainly the duke, his serfs, and a portly little boy who said, "I don't think Trump is really a conservative, since he's a girl and a Jew."

Jane turned off the radio and lit a Parliament. "I'm gonna kill us all and fuck the world," she said. She traced an invisible line around Jesse's body with her finger. "Ze wasn't killed here. This metaphor has the clarity of a warbler hatching under a new moon."

"I wouldn't be surprised to see more. Say the scene had the stillness of a midnight Klan prayer, relics raising the offspring rendition, definitively staged, foreign born, a real Malibu type," Jack said. "The light . . ."

"That's a wrap," said Jane. "Strip the lens coating, then find me video with more angle on hir face, a considerable thread of alt-brightness."

"No kidding," said Jack. "You cool with me sending hir DNA to the Donald? The tox screen will go automatically anyway, but this way we can handle the whole case a-crawlin' in his lousy smokehouse."

"Honeylamb," Jane said, "you ain't seen nothing yet."

IV. Road to Nowhere

America is a mistake. A gigantic mistake. —Sigmund Freud

How it all started was Charlie and I.

Start over.

How it all started was Charlie and me. Me and Charlie was.

Start over.

What happened was we were driving out across Wyoming.

We was. We were, we was. We was. We was drivin cross somewheres. What happened was we was drivin cross the country, somewheres in Wyomin. Start over.

Wrapping sausages in first one, then two and three napkins, absentmindedly half watching the blonde woman's flat-screen jaw flop out the morning All the News You Need for Your Day War with China? Superhurricane Melania Tampa Evacuation Gas Shortage, she didn't see the man walking toward her across the mostly empty restaurant until he was standing over her with his tray, Peterbilt hat, and goofy smile. He said something and she looked up, past the gravy and hash browns, taking him in, ready to ignore, bolt, or step-pull-jab as necessary. Here I am, she thought, hunched over my coffee in my ratty Cattle Decapitation shirt and clunky hipster frames, red eyed and greasy haired, I thought I had my fuck-off face on.

"Mind if I sit down?" he asked, maybe the second time,

she wasn't sure. He had on those black steel-toed sneakers security guards wore.

A glance at the extensive selection of empty tables, communicating what, indulgence? Or briefly, why? He had nice eyes, at least, and seemed friendly, despite the oddness of approaching a stranger at the Chuck Wagon Buffet at seven o'clock in the A.M., so she shrugged slightly more than not at all.

He sat down with his tray and took off his ball cap, revealing a smooth brown helmet of hat hair lengthening to a tidy mullet at the back. Five o'clock shadow and wry blue eyes. She didn't say anything.

"Not from here, are you?" he said, grinning.

"Weak opening," she said flatly, resuming wrapping sausages in total practiced nonchalance.

"Sorry, I don't mean to hassle you. I just saw you over here on your own and thought a pretty girl like you might like company."

"You do a lot of cruising at the Chuck Wagon? That what passes for Tinder out here?"

He laughed, the sound of dusty boots in open air, a laugh that seemed to need a knee slap to complete it. "I work the night shift at the prison," he said, "so I come by here a lot for dinner. Or breakfast. I don't usually pick up women, but I saw your Cattle Decapitation T-shirt and figured, hey, any lady who's into eco-radical deathgrind must at least be interesting to talk to . . ."

"Don't imagine they play out here much," she said, sliding the wrapped sausages off the table and into her bag. He work at a prison? For real? Be careful not to seem any warmer than suspicious, or the fucker might get ideas. Frankly, the whole trip had been a freak show from the beginning, from the first Pennsylvania pit stop with one-eyed "Chiyanne" behind the counter all the way to last night's *Survivor: Extreme Weather* film crew at the Best Western, and what kind of name is Chiyanne anyway, printed all caps on a white sticky label? Is it, like, phonetic? And why here, why *Extreme Weather*? Did they know something she didn't? Not mentioning the StormWatch convoy that passed her outside Elkhart, a different kind of climate change: four up-armored Humvees with turret-mounted machine guns and Indiana Civil Defense tags, one with a #QANON bumper sticker.

"I saw 'em when they came through Fargo a few years back, for the Karma.Bloody.Karma tour," he said. "There's a lot of metal fans out here, you'd be surprised." Still smiling, digging into his eggs and gravy now. He reminded her vaguely of this pimpled jock she'd macked on in high school who, when she pulled his dick out of his pants in the back of his car, had exclaimed: "Whoa, I thought you were a dyke."

"Not so much."

He shook his head. "Naw, really, there's lots of metalheads out here. Fewer vegetarians, it's true," he said wistfully, picking up a forkful of gravy-coated eggs.

"That"—time to go—"I don't doubt, but rather my surprise. Look, Mr.—?"

"Mike. Call me Mike."

"Look, Mr. Mike, I got miles to go before I sleep. The Fergus Falls Chuck Wagon is peachy keen, but I must needs hit the road. Hope you don't think I'm rude."

"Well, uh, I don't even know your name, ah, I mean, where you goin' in such a hurry?"

She stood with her bag and leaned over the table—"Tell 'em Suzie sent ya"—then rapped a knuckle twice on the grease-flecked laminate and spun in her low-cut Cons, sweeping past the buffet and out the door, not looking behind, not looking anywhere but out to the car in the lot waiting against the low green of west Minnesota, the massed clouds looking suspiciously like tornado weather, and her Jack Russell Abelard standing against the driver's side window with his snout dug into the crack and snapping ceaselessly, his pink tongue curling like a tentacle, just like he'd been when she left him. He was a dependable little shitface.

Leaving had not been a hard decision, as such decisions go. Ever since getting back in fact from that bullshit clusterfuck road movie and collecting Steve the Cat from Cathy, a niggling itch grew by night, plains invading her dreams, space and air calling *Suzie*, and day by day she struggled and failed to remember why the hell she loved New York, what she wanted, how it all worked. The UberATs *will* stop for you, that's the way it is, it's not something wrong with them when they edge and push and seem about to ever so slowly run you over simply by not stopping, no, they'll stop, there are *rules* here, but what the fuck, why bother? It didn't help that Remy had turned spastic, calling at weird hours, carrying some sort of guilt for what had happened. She told him take your baggage to JFK, honeylamb, 'cause there ain't no room for it here.

It was Steve running away—she almost said "escaped"— that clinched it. Fine, she thought, now the one human being I can depend on in the world is gone and he was a cat, so fuck it, I'll apply somewhere out there, some fucking Buckeye Podunk State College, Flyover U, anything away for a new start, a real new start, start over for real. With her New York grit and crabby glare she'd be unique, a character, instant personality, and it would give her time to adjust to whatever song she'd find playing when the record flipped.

So she applied to MFAs across the land, playing nice in class to get her recommendations, trying to work what happened with Jim and Remy into something worthwhile and failing, some road movie novel, then writing other stuff, some other things, the last one she's working now in scraps and bits, *The True Life Story of the Highway Killers*, or *Charlie and Me*, or maybe *Caril Ann's Last Stand*, driving it across the country in a stained green Mead notebook, working up the fake to take the edge off the real, trying not to remember so hard all the people she was leaving behind, trying to bundle and sink old memories of, for instance, Nate the sk8r boi, with the pale chin scar and orange-spotted brown eyes always wide open like he was gonna jump, such a sweet guy and when he showed up bleeding knees and elbows asking "You gotta Band-Aid?" she knew he'd be hard to unhook. Packing/throwing away her life to fit the remains into her new used car, she'd found boxes and boxes of gauze and tape and tubes of Neosporin, and it was all she wanted in the world to punch his number into her cell and hear his lopey fragments, Sup, yeah, hey bro, but no, she just smiled, and now, crossing Fargo in the butter-gold light of a Great Plains morning, America bang-flat before her sea to sea, driving into the coming storm, she let herself linger on his really quite enormous nose and crooked cock, his lean waist and huge feet, his shyness, tenderness, and sulky humors. She remembers he dumped her by text message.

How many fresh starts you get? Like a deck of inky-blue cards, little pictures, draw and play—she had a feeling she was getting near the bottom, though, like whatever's next better stick.

"What you think, Abelard?" she asked the curled white tube on the passenger seat snoring softly. His ear twitched in post-sausage stupor.

At this point she could only imagine the blue Rockies in the distance, because from here it was still miles of miles, Fargo left behind and Valley City, Jamestown, and Bismarck yet to break, rolling and humming and thick air whistling in the window, oldies, classic rock, country, Today's Urban Beats, All Polka All the Time, *Live from Here*. These northly, arid plains were different from the OK scrub she knew in her blood, yet gave the world the same sense of infinity, the far-curved horizon, endless sky, immensities of brown and blue and gray making you see yourself a spot dribbled onto eternity, a little nothing that happened once and was gone the next fall. The exact obverse of New York, where the world is a hum happening only for you. And not just the flat but the lack, the emptiness of it, the absence of human growth—not that there's no formation, Costcos and Sinclairs, for example, the highway, but here the structure seemed temporary against eons of earth and wind, while in NYC the present is all there is, built up on a granite spar you don't even think about.

It was the sense of inevitability she remembered from the

plains that troubled her most, a sense that came from how easy it was to cast lives adrift on the flats, how shallow roots dug here. If it wasn't flooding or tornadoes, then it was a freak storm smashing trees into houses or drought or a late frost choking the first shoots of spring or a hailstorm crippling the harvest, not that she ever lived on a farm but that was how it was in her imagination, fed on Laura Ingalls Wilder and Willa Cather and *The Wizard of Oz*, the texture of being out here, or maybe just her mind, a recurring melody that sang "vanitas, vanitas," backed by the whipsaw rhythms of the Dust God's steel pedal guitar. Tomorrow would come because the storm clouds would always build on the horizon and sweep the day down, tomorrow would come because killing winter would always freeze, tomorrow would come because the brutal son would always rise, tomorrow would come down onto the plains like death because that was what it did, but you might not be there to meet it. You were trash to be swept up in a crosswind, twisted into space, and tossed away, again and again, ashes to ashes, dust to dust.

How it all started was like this.

It started out Charlie and me fell in love.

Start over.

What happened was we were driving out across Wyoming.

We was drivin out acrost. Acrossed. Acrosst. Across't? Cross. We was drivin cross Wyomin. What happened. Happind. What happind wuz we wuz drivin cross. Start over.

She lit a Parliament and cracked the window, somewhere out there, later, while tornado-storm rain turned the road to white water, her destination the other side of the veil.

She'd applied to various programs, got into a few, and had eventually decided on Seattle. She had looked, looked, and looked, peering into photos on websites for answers to her questions: who were these people, what would it be like, what did the future hold. She was baffled by the notion that she recognized almost none of the names anywhere, yet all the bios claimed novels written, poetry published, awards won, articles and stories in the *New Yorker* and *Tin House*.

She said writing was the important thing, of course, that was the party line, but really? For fuck's sake. Everyone talked like it was religion, like you were touched by the Holy Spirit because you liked to tell stories or thought words were cool. Artaud was closer to the truth when he said all writing is shit and all writers pigs. Inspiration? Craft? Try ego. Try delusion. Try pettiness and ressentiment. All these twisted perverts taking out bent passions on a blank page, making shit up, inventing lies, a bunch of fuckups spending their nights muttering to themselves over their laptops.

She stopped writing and looked up at Abelard and Abelard looked up at her. I stopped writing, she wrote, I wrote she stopped writing. Go back and read it again. She turned where she sat with her back to the window, the dog on the bed, the dark screen, she turned her head to face the uncurtained window pounded by the storm's rain, the weird storm glow casting her in fuzzed-out silhouette, gray on gray, and she saw herself reflected in the screen and Abelard's gaze, remembering someone writing about how the miraculous quality in Rembrandt was in the way he caught figures just as they turned toward the light.

It was the collection of Day-Glo silicon yard gnomes at

the New Museum, standing Gulliverian among the rotund
mini orgiasts bent in pink and yellow erotic convolutions,
this one holding her breasts up around her beard, this one
spreading its ass to the sky, this one sticking all its fingers
from both hands in its mouth, boy-girls, girl-boys, bearded
women and lady-men in pairs, triads, and garden-gnome
daisy chains, neon blue and green and orange, fucking and
sucking one another's beards and cocks and cunts and tits
and assholes, heigh-ho, heigh-ho, dig dig dig the utopian
art-commodity dullness of it all, feeling as she flâneured
through disgraced and bored and gazing out the gallery
windows at the light descending through the sky over the
city like the fall of heaven, smears of molten cloud and
a plane crossing, a gently arcing black star, remembering
when Bowie died and that P J Harvey song about a rooftop
in Brooklyn and seeing Melt-Banana play the Williamsburg Music Hall and watching Lou Reed fall asleep at a
Richard Foreman show at St. Marks and CBGB closing
down and the Dunkin' Donuts going in at the corner of
Bedford and Seventh that had finally put the last piece
in the deterritorialization puzzle that had for weeks been
quietly assembling itself within her, the message now as
obvious as Kara Walker at the Domino Sugar Factory. That
was after Steve fled and before she got Abelard, around the
same time her mother got cancer. Now, quiet in a hotel
somewhere in America, she writes I am sitting in a room
writing about thinking about remembering, my dog's looking at me, the rain's washing out the highway, we're taking
the Oregon Trail out West, what dusty life, dysentery and
Indians, I was trapped in a Koons now I'm trapped in a

Hopper, still the same soulless gape, alone in a room with a screen.

And a dog.

And Charlie.

Start over.

And how it all started was me and Charlie fell in love. How it all started was a movie. How it all started was Jim called and Charlie was.

Start over.

It started out Charlie and me—start over.

What happened was we was driving out across Wyomin.

She counts light poles by the roadside. She pounces on the page. There's an emptiness across the land, across her mind, a blank scrawl, cataract sky, inhospitable fallowness, dead mammals, reflections in glass wiped flat by time. Extinction time, end time, first time. She crosses the country and lives happily ever after, gets her MFA, teaches creative writing. She writes a road movie, she writes the true story of Caril Ann Fugate, she writes a hundred books about dead and made-up people.

Return, tab, type.

Start over.

What happind wuz.

The emptiness should be the page and not the language. The emptiness should be breath. I never wanted any of this, she thinks, I never wanted to come here and I never wanted to go, I just wanted something different. But what's that even mean? What's different? How is anything different from anything else? I just wanted a new start, start over. I didn't want the thing but wanted not the thing that was, the unthing, another thing, a future unformed by the past. I wanted *nothing*. Where do they sell *nothing*?

Return, tab, type.

Me and Charlie.

Disconnect, destroy, liberate, occupy, break free from this toil of endless days, summon the Wind Son, unleash the Anthropocene, a new glory, always fresh, but that's not what happens, is it? In fact it's scar tissue and bad reactions, sleepless nights, accumulation and wreckage.

Return, tab, type.

Start over.

I wanted nothing. *Nothing*. How fucking hard is it to get a little nothing?

The mountains show the next morning, a blue haze on the horizon that as she drives resolves into distant peaks, the world washed clean by rain. Curving into rise, not geology but geometry, the edge of the plane.

"I see them there," she says to Abelard, who looks up at her, head cocked, "and it's the same as it was before, going the other way. I mean, the sense of leaving, being free, it's in the plains maybe, I don't know. I never felt free in New York. I felt hemmed in, beleaguered, bothered, rattrapped, and wasted time, always something doing, and then after a certain point that seemed normal, like what we were. I don't know. It was a good tour, Toto. I wish I could have said goodbye to Steve."

She looked down at Abelard, who was munching on his crotch, and shook her head.

She lit another Parliament and cracked the window. The smoke in her lungs came down with savory pain. But if you start by saying no, then what do you have left? Former model, former wage-slave office drone, clockwatcher, paper shuffler, former New Yorker of SoHo, the LES, and Flatbush-a.k.a.-Ridgewood, messy, smoking, no doubt cancerous, flabby but still thin enough, needs more and more product to manage her face, snappy, hip, prickly, uncongenial, doesn't like people, likes animals but not enough to be a vegetarian, a hater who takes ambivalent pleasure in the end of human civilization, the fall of America, should have been a nun, like Teresa de Ávila, should have found her ecstasy in God but instead smeared it across a decade of bad calls, questionable liaisons, and date-rapey sex. Can you retire at forty? Onward to the next lucky break, Abelard, some new thing to hate. They got whales out there, kid, sharks, too, even if they're all suffering debilitating hormonal failure from the toxins leaching into the sea.

When I was growing up, I wanted to live in a Jane's Addiction video. Now? Dad sitting there in his favorite chair, wearing his dress blues with his medals all over his chest, flattop haircut and ruddy cheeks, and Mom lying in a hospital bed with chrome rails, hooked to an IV, her life leaking out in slow breaths. Green-bean tater-tot casserole on the counter, cream of mushroom soup and ground beef. The TV's playing Fox News with the sound off, the only other light the dimmed sun seeping through the closed blinds shutting out the sliding glass door at the back. The hi-fi's playing Roger Miller, "Lock, Stock and Teardrops," with that creepazoid electro-voice backing him and the slow boom-chicka-boom, meanwhile the EKG beeps, the IV drips, dad lifts his arm and sips his bourbon. He's got

those cheap black shiny air-force dress shoes on, he's looking into space, and over his shoulder in the weak gleam
float constellations of transient dust, universes of mote life
swirling.

She saw the sign for the rest area and pulled off. She put
Abelard's leash on and got him up and out into the yellow-
ing grass. The rest area was nearly empty, only one other
car, towels hanging in the windows to keep the sun out, and
nobody else around. Abelard pulled the extender out to the
max, sniffing at something, then threw himself on his back
in the fine brown dirt.

The mountains were bigger now, weighty in the distance, massive and gray. She was finally feeling the end of
the prairie, the earth was rising into solemn humps, and the
mountains lent the drive a sense of narrative, some chap-
tered sequence, repetition and change.

"Pee already," she said, drinking water from her bottle.
Then she noticed a round-eyed pale boy with a cowlick
watching her from the window of the other car, maybe six
or seven years old, staring with that blue intensity lonely
children have, open and probing, making her feel as if she'd
somehow exposed herself. Thankfully, Abelard was straining out a turd cluster, so she didn't have to stand there being
stared at long before they got back in the car and drove off.

Abelard barked at nothing.

Later, sitting by the fire and feeding him a hot dog, she
thought back through the pines and campground and was
filled with an unexpected sense of loss. Not for anyone
in particular, not for Jim or Steve or New York or Dad,
but something vague and structural in the sense of parties

meeting and slipping away, the contingency of it all, sudden clashes and moves in disparate space, like without Oklahoma there was nothing, which is ridiculous, she knows. She had people in New York, contacts, longtime friends, but then, there, honestly, it was one thing and then another and was there anyone she still knew from the old days? And did she ever really care? The city was so far behind now, all the way across the country, back through the mountain passes in the dark night, back through the trees, invisible, glowing, waiting there at the edge of the continent, a sprinkle of lights over a stab of black schist, seawalled sprawl at the edge of America, and what did it have to do with her, or she with it? Much as she'd left Oklahoma behind, turning her back on the width and breadth of Middle American plainness, she'd now turned her back on New York, on the starry-eyed hubris of the Empire State and the mad scramble up the maze, the dumb clutch at the brass ring, the money and greed and ambition and exception that powered the city in waves of mindless faddishness, but she couldn't turn her back on America, could she, still here, still her, still making its way down the new century that already felt so terribly old. And west? What was west?

It's where you start over.

Abelard looked up and she absentmindedly fed him another bit of hot dog, thinking about these last few days, years, this life, Jim and Remy and Jim's fierce dream and crazy escape—rupture? evasion?—and how she'd never lost the sense she had of something mysterious coming to life when he'd stood there in the bar and opened his map across the table, giving them the nation at a glance, its secrets and

truths plotted across the grid in blue rivers and lines of rising peaks, flyover junctions and suburbanized metropoles,
nowheres and dreamlands, hints scrawled in crazed graf-
fiti, and how at the same time the map meant it was there,
there it was, given and pre-owned, already been chewed,
and even for all that space, there was a way you couldn't go
anywhere anymore, somehow, where they weren't already
looking. It'd all been fenced off. And what this had to do
with Caril Fugate and Charlie Starkweather, with guns and
the Sinaloan War and Whitman and Trump and Oklahoma
City, how somehow it all meant something she couldn't
quite grasp, couldn't quite put her finger on, something big
and important and dying, maybe already dead, and how her
chest seemed to open at the pain of the past and the promise of tomorrow, the clear impossible anything rising in the
sky, the great big lie she still wanted to believe in, her lover,
America, the road.

That's why, typing at the hotel the next night at the edge
of the edge of the mountains, almost there now, that's why
this now, the screen, that's why she exists, why she thinks
and breathes and talks, why she's heading across the country writing heading across the country, why there's a second
life, why another life, why you start with The Word, why
the word was, why the word was in the beginning, why you
start over, that's why she types *what happened was*, but no,
that's not right. Start over.

What happened was.

How it all started was like this.

It started out with Charlie and I.

Start over.

Charlie and me. Start over.

What happened was that we were driving out across Wyoming.

We were, we was. We was drivin cross somewheres. What happened was we was drivin out across the country, somewheres in Wyoming. Start over.

What happind was, we was on a lonely stretch a road somewheres in Wyomin and it was the first time I'd ever seen the mountains ever, all dark and high against the edge of the prairie and I thought how we got to go over them, there ain't no way, and I felt sad and angry cause we knowed they was after us, we heard all about us on the radio.

Start over. Do it again.

What happind was we was on a lonely stretch a road somewheres in Wyomin and it was the first time I'd seed the mountains ever, all dark and high against the edge of the prairie, and I thought how we gotta go over em, there ain't no way I thought, and I's sad and angry cause I knowed they's after us, we heard all about us on the radio, and Charlie says they knowed what kinda car we had and he said they's looking for us for sure now, so we stops at this car, I think it's a Buick, just out on the road and Charlie gets out and walks up like a big sheriff and all that like he always done and I sees him talking to the man in the car but he won't open the winder so Charlie comes back and he gets the twenty-two and takes it and shoots in the winder and shoots the man again must a been ten times. I reckon he just went crazy. I thought, he just gone crazy and got all scared cuz a last night he made me do it with him when I didn't want to so I thought what if he tries somethin now and he's all crazy? That's why I got outta the car when that man come by. First there's the one man who drove by and turned around and come back and I thought Charlie you better shoot him too and he gets outta the car and walks up and Charlie points a gun at him and the man grabs it and they start rasslin then that deputy come up in his car and I run up to him and says, "Take me to the police," and he says, "Get in," so I did, then I tole him how Charlie killed a man there and he asks me who that is and I just looked at him funny and said: "That there's Charlie Starkweather."

I member at the beginnin when he tole me he killed Bob Colvert, he said some others done it but I knowed right away he was the one cuz even if he was scared he couldn't help but make a little grin like he done something bad, and he took me and we drove around town and I made him tell me all about it, how he said he walked right in with his shotgun and said you just put that money in that bag there then he made Bob drive him out by Bloody Mary's where he said he was just gonna leave him tied up but Bob tried to hit him and grab the gun so he just shot him bang like that. He said it was awful cold and dark, it being December and all, and nighttime, and I asks him what's it feel like killing a man and he says it feels good, real good, like its the first right thing I ever done. And I says the second right thing, you dog, and gives him a kiss him on the cheek. Then we parked and he kissed me up some and he asks me you want to touch the gun and I say yes, and he takes it out from under the seat and I look at it and thought, that's how you kill a man right there, with some black metal, just a piece of the world like a tool or a hammer, and that's how Charlie done Bob Colvert. He just took him out and shot him like a dog.

When Charlie dropped me off at home my ma come at me soon as I was back sayin "Where you been with that Charlie Starkweather" and "I don't know what you two do driving around in his car but it ain't right and you better watch out," nagging on me and making it sound like me and Charlie was the worst sinners in all Nebraska, like there weren't a hunnerd other kids running around doing worse'n us, and I wanted a tell her "You don't even know what we're doing, you old hag, you don't even know what we do!" I wanted a tell her, "Charlie just killed a man, you dried-up nasty witch, what you think a that? Howabout we kill you?" I didn't say it, a course, I wanted to, and then later on we did. Charlie shot her in her stupid pinched-up old face but she wasn't dead yet, so then he smashed in her head with his rifle. That was later on, though, and I never told anyone nor will I ever but I don't mind saying now even for all the years I spent at York which weren't so bad oncet you got used to it, I'm glad he done it, glad he went and shot her cuz she was a mean old nasty hag who needed somebody to shoot her five or ten times even. It ain't so's you could shoot her enough to be done with her what she needed done to her. And he killed Marion too and he had it coming that sumbitch and I'll tell you about that when I comes to it but that day, I mean to say, after Charlie tole me he done killed Bob Colvert, I member coming in the parlor room and Marion's watching TV and fixing at some business, one a his projects like he was always working on, this thing-amajig he had all apart with a screwdriver and was trying to fix it, doing tiny little work with his big old hands, like one of them giants from a story trying to make something normal size, and I stood in the door looking at him and Betty Jean on the floor and the man on the TV was talking about how Russian Sputnik fell right outta the sky into the Pacific Ocean and he says how folks in California saw it fallin t'other night and thought it were a UFO like in the movies but it weren't, it were just them Russians spreading their Communist lies.

I thought about that and how it seemed real beautiful to me cuz I seen shooting stars before, and to watch it burn and slide across the sky like a smeary trail a golden red falling from space like the bloody tears a heaven, it must a been beautiful, Commie or not, it don't matter if it were Chinese or if it really were a UFO like they thought, it must a been glorious. You don't get to see something like that all the time in a life. A life ain't such a long thing and it ain't so full of beauty neither, it's mostly dumb bossy people yelling at you and cold winters and things you thought would happen that turn out wrong, but if you get something beautiful like that you oughta hang on to it.

Like after we killed all them and we were living in the house just Charlie and me, we was just kids then but it was like our honeymoon, real beautiful 'cept for him wanting to do it all the time. But I ain't even there yet. First we had the money he took from Bob Colvert and the gas station and he bought candy and sodas for me, he took me to the pitchers most every day that week, we saw *The Parson and the Outlaw* and *Escape from San Quentin* and we saw *Man in the Shadow* and *Last of the Badmen* and *Pickup Alley* and

Domino Kid, we'd go see a pitcher then go back and sit in Charlie's room and he'd say the lines from the pitcher in his mirror and practice drawing a gun like he's a big sheriff, and I told him "You look just like him, Charlie. Just like." Those was beautiful times too, I member, fore everything got confused, and we'd sit in his room drawing pitchers and eating candies and then he'd practice his knife throwin, just like them Indians did, he said a friend of his knowed a real Indian who tole him the secrets a throwin knives.

He wanted to do it real bad all the time but I tole him we wasn't married yet so all I let him do was stick it in a inch was all, and if he was gonna make milk he had to do it on the floor or in his hand. He was real sore bout that but it hurt real bad, even a inch, and also I weren't gon have no baby, not with us not even being married in the eyes of the Lord, but it didn't matter anyway cuz everbody thought we was doing it like two little sinners, my ma was at me and Marion too and at last they tole me not to see him no more, so one day I comes home from school and most days Charlie waits for me and I go with him but I din't see him that day till I was nearly home and I knowed they was prolly watching me so I din't talk to him but came around and Nig was barking like nothing and it must a been Charlie he was barking at and I come in and Ma says "Where you been at?" and I says "School" but what I want a say is "Why don't you go die, you nasty old witch?" Then she says "Charlie been around and he's acting all funny, and Marion says he can't come around no more." I says "You can't do that we're in love," and she says "I bet you are you little harlot, I bet you know all about being in love with

Charlie Starkweather," and I says "You don't know nothin bout nothin'," and she says "Look here Miss Mouth, you better watch who you're talking to or you'll get some of what I gave Charlie. It's bad enough you got knocked up, we don't need him messing around" and I says "I ain't pregnant, Ma, we ain't done nothing," and she says "Don't try to tell me what I see, you little hussy, I know a baby belly when I see one, and you listen here, Marion tole him he can't never see you again and the same goes for you" and then I says "It ain't like that" and that's when Charlie comes in the screen door and Ma says "There's the little egg-sucking dog right now. How you like knocking up little girls, huh, mister?"

Well he just looked at her real mean-like and says "I ain't come to talk" and she says "I thought I told you not to come around here" then she ups and slaps him in the face, just like that, and he grabs her and hits her back and a chair gets knocked over and she starts screaming like a crazy woman, then Marion come in saying you little so-and-so and grabs him to throw him out the door but Charlie rassles him and they wind up on the floor shoving and hitting each other and Marion pushes Charlie off and gets up and goes off then Charlie goes off too and I follered em into the parlor where Betty Jean was playing on the floor and then I sees Charlie come back with a twenty-two and then Marion comes back in the front door, the front door what was really in the back, what we used, in our yard out to the street, but we always went in and out the kitchen door in the back what was by the gravel lane, but then Marion comes in and he got a clawhammer in his hand and blood in his eye like he finally gonna give Charlie what he thought and I screamed "No,

Charlie," and that's when Charlie shot him in the head. He stopped where he was and looked at us mean as cuss but kinda confused and then fell right down on the dresser, he dropped the hammer and fell over like he was dead. Then Ma comes in with a kitchen knife saying "I'm gonna kill you, Charlie Starkweather," and I says "No, Ma, no!" and Charlie backed up toward Marion and did something with his gun and I grabbed at Ma saying "No, don't," and she slapped me in the head and knocked me over then Charlie shot her right in her dumb old witch face. Bang! She kinda tripped over herself and looked around, then she looked over at Betty Jean and started walking across the room, and Charlie just stared at her, still pointing his gun, and she looked at Betty Jean and fell right over. Then she rolled over and looked up at him and his face turned all bad like he was gonna puke his guts up and he smashed her head with the butt of his rifle. That's when I realized Betty Jean was crying like she always does, god I hated her crying like a little meanie so I says "Shut up!" and Charlie looked over at me then at Betty Jean then went over and hit her in the head too and she fell over and shut up. I saw Marion still moving then so I got the knife Ma had and went over and stabbed him in the neck hard, but the knife wouldn't go in far so I hit it with my hand then moved it around back and forth in his neck, like when you can't get the joint in a chicken, trying to cut him up inside, and he was making funny noises in his mouth like a hiss and a chuckle and his eyes was looking at me and he was bleeding all over and I dug that knife in, moving it around in his neck, thinking you die you dirty sumbitch. Charlie just stood there looking at me and I got up and went over to Betty Jean cuz I didn't want her to wake up so I stabbed her in the neck, too, and I turned and said "Look at what you done, Charlie Starkweather!"

Betty Jean was only two and a half and she was the nastiest little thing you ever saw in your life, always screaming and in your business, always messing herself and sticking her fingers in everything.

Weren't no good in any of em, nothing worth saving on this world or in heaven, and Charlie did the right thing even though at the time I was awful sore at him for making a mess, and I's scared and angry and I din't know what was gonna happen. I says to him "What are we gonna do now, Charlie?" and he says "I don't know, let me think" he says, then he sets his gun down and goes and turns on the TV and sets down in Marion's chair. I member the *Mickey Mouse Club* was on and it was Monday so it was Fun with Music Day and they was singing songs and seemed so happy and cheerful. Charlie wouldn't normally watch Mickey Mouse cuz that's just kids' stuff he'd say, but he sat there staring at the TV and I went and set on the love seat watching too then they had on "Walt Disney Presents: Annette," which was a part of the show, all about this country girl name Annette what was Annette Funicello, who was what Marion called a guinea broad, and she was from the country like us but she moved to a big city with her hoity-toity aunt and uncle, who was saying "You must use your *dessert* spoon for dessert, you silly girl." I laughed some, cuz even though it was kid stuff it was still funny, and when Charlie heard me laugh he looked over like he'd slap me upside the head but then he laughed too, and we both laughed and looked at each other, then we watched some more TV. After that show was over there was a cowboy show on and we watched that then it was dark outside, so Charlie said he might as well clean up the mess he made. When he got up he pointed at two pieces a carpet by the dresser and says "I brought them over for your ma but she din't even say thank you. I thought she'd like em, and they was free cause they was samples I took off the wood, and I brought em over and all she said was 'You can't see Caril no more.' What kinda thanks is that?"

"You scared for what you done?" I asks him.

"Naw, I ain't scared" he says.

"What a we do?" I asks him.

"I don't know" he says "but I know Marion Bartlett ain't gon stand between you and me no more. You and me's free as scouts on a prairie."

Truth tole I don't think he went crazy when he shot that man in Wyomin. I ain't never tole no one the truth bout what happind, not the whole thing, and I ain't never tole no one what I done or ain't done, and sometime thinking back it gets confused, cuz sometimes I know I done things and other times I think I din't do that, I can't a done that, that was Charlie. Like how I just tole you I stuck a knife in Marion's neck, I just membered it was Charlie done that, not me. Wasn't me. I din't do that.

But that day when he shot that man in Wyomin, I din't think Charlie was crazy at all, at least no more than he was already, not since that first day, but he kept wanting to do it and then he was doing it with all them other women and I knowed he couldn't get us over them mountains, I knowed we was caught, and I thought my one true and only hope is to tell the deputy that's Charlie and he kidnapped me the whole time. Charlie was a dirty little sneak and he kept doing them other women and I'd kill him right now myself he came here today and he weren't already dead, I'd kill him and stab him in his neck and shoot him in his dirty face, stupid bowlegged sumbitch, I'd kill him to death. I'm glad he got his, frying in that chair, cuz he was a dirty little egg-sucking runt and needed to die, which if I'd a known then, when it started, I'd a just shot him too and said he killed everyone, officer, then shot hisself, he just went crazy, but when he killed Ma and Marion and Betty Jean I thought he's a big sheriff and I thought he's real brave and strong to do all that killing.

Just goes to show you never know how things'll turn out.

Anyway that day he drug all em out to the outhouse and we cleaned up the blood all on the floor, but there's still this thick smell a blood all over so I got some a Ma's perfume and sprinkled it all on the floor. Then after that we took Marion's money and went over by Hutson's Grocery and got some Pepsi-Cola and a big bag a tater chips, and we came back and watched some more TV till we fell asleep. I remember waking up in the night and seeing the station gone off and the TV screen just static, filling up the room with a gray and ghostly light, and for a minute I forgot what happened and I looked around like we was gonna get caught cuz Charlie was laying curled up on me, then I membered that they was all dead and in the outhouse and I was scared for a minute cuz a dead body's got something in it that'll scare you if you think about it too long, then I thought how brave Charlie was shooting my ma in the face like that and I thought, here's a good man'll protect me in all the perils a life to come.

We had Nig our black dog and a new collie puppy what we named Kim, and we had two parakeets, too, and we got ice cream and candy and chips and more soda pop, and we stayed there in that house like it was a honeymoon, we played gin rummy and watched *The Thin Man* and Abbott and Costello on TV, and Charlie practiced his knife throwin. It a been perfect, we din't have nobody tell us do this or that, we din't have nobody in our business or telling us what's what, we just talked all about our dreams and hopes, and we talked about how we'd get out to Montana or maybe Washington, Charlie had a uncle out Washington way said he'd give us some land to build our home and future on, Charlie went on and on about what it meant for a man to have some space and freedom, just a little space to call his own and not be beholden to these sumbitches who're always at you and telling you what to do, he just wanted a cabin in the mountains where the air was clean, and we'd have some horses and chickens and goats, and he'd ranch out cattle and chop wood and I'd take care of the farm and kids, just like the olden days, just like it was supposed to be. He done made himself out to be some kinda rebel in the news, fore they fried him, he made hisself out just like he wanted to be famous and have a big name, and it's true he talked about how they'd all talk about Charlie Starkweather, no mistakin that, he wanted people to know his name and know he was trouble from the word go, but that was just him all acting up the big sheriff, cuz

I swear all he wanted was to be let alone, just have his space and be free and let alone, just have somewheres just for us, someplace we could call our own out on the frontier, out West somewheres, someplace what belonged to us and us alone, and we talked up all about what kinda wood we'd use for the cabin and what the names of our chickens would be and what we'd name our little ones, we talked it all up and it a been perfect that week in the house exceptin that people kept coming by, and we had a tell em stay away Ma's sick, we all had the five-day flu is what we said, me at the door and Charlie hidden back in the house so's they wouldn't see him, and asides from the people bothering us there was Charlie and his damned little thing, him always working it up and wanting to put it in me, and I told him not till we's married just a inch, and he said we's married now in the eyes of God, he says, and I says I don't want no baby yet till we get to Montana, so he says if he puts it in my mouth it don't make no babies at all so I said that's dirty and you're a dirty dog, but I milked him off with my hand, which was dirty but better than when he put it in me, even just a inch, which always burned like a devil, and he'd be kissing on me and grabbing at me, but I din't want nothing to do with it and I hated it and hated him just like I hated Marion, just like I hated being touched all the time, I never took my clothes off and I hated him touching me and wanting me to do it all the time, but it made him so pleased with hisself I couldn't say no so I milked him off, and then him and me was both happy cuz he got his and I din't have to let him put it in me where it hurt and make no babies, and I never had a take my clothes off cuz he was the dirty one who did the dirty things, he was the bad one who wanted a do nasty things, not me, it weren't me that wanted none of it I just hated it, hated it and hated him for what he done. I hated him then and I do today and I did when he did them other women, too, and I hated them for doin it with him, I wanted to kill em all, them and him and Marion all dead and stabbed and I'd stab em in the neck and in their nasties and in their belly and stab em till they couldn't never do it no more, ain't no reason why people should ever do it cept having babies and that's a big mean joke from God, it's our sin and burden, that we gotta be dirty animals what make babies, and I shouldn't even be talking about it now, not to you and not ever.

Suzie looked down at Abelard sleeping, then out the window, then back at the notebook. She wondered what exactly had happened to Caril, and how close she had to go to keep her real and breathing. Caril didn't really want to remember anything, she didn't want to know, and that was part of what she was getting into, that was part of the conceit here, because in real life Caril had said she was innocent the whole time. In real life Caril said "I don't remember what went on in that house."

"What do you mean, Caril?" she was asked.

"I don't remember it at all."

"You don't remember it at all?"

"I don't remember it at all."

"What do you mean, you don't remember it at all?"

"I don't remember what went on."

"Can you remember what you told me, when you talked to me?"

"I don't remember."

But she did. We do.

You remember, don't you? You remember what happened?

I member them days we lived like kings and queens exceptin for people coming by all the time. Barbara and her stupid husband Bob Von Busch kept coming by, then Bob and Charlie's brother called the police, who come by then left. All them people coming by was making us nervous, specially them police on Saturday night, and we had a nice big day on Sunday cuz nobody came by but then Monday my granny Pansy come by and wouldn't leave, she kep on shouting and trying to open the door, and I tole her you gotta go away granny we got the five-day flu but she wouldn't listen, then she said "I know you got that Charlie in there and you're doing something, and I'm coming back here with the police."

Well that was the end a our beautiful honeymoon and we left. Charlie took Marion's pistol and a shotgun wrapped up in a blue blanket and I took my red swim bag what I could fit some things in, and we each took a knife and I took some old pitchers of me and Barbara and friends a mine what I wouldn't never see again and it made me kinda sad lookin at them pitchers thinkin how I din't even get to say goodbye or have Christmas but how it was all cuz I was gonna spend my future with Charlie in the woods and we'd be happy and safe all by ourselves, how we'd get to start over and have a whole new life a freedom.

Anyways before getting on the road we had to go get

Charlie's car and change a bad tire, then we went to Crest I think it was where we got gas and some maps, and then we went to the garage he rented so he could get some spare tires cuz he said we might need em. Charlie loved his car but it was having problems then, that one tire had a bad rim on it and he had a bad transmission too, so he says to me we gotta stop somewhere and get it fixed. The tire was wobblin too much to drive on so we went to Dale's or Tate's, one of em first I don't member which, where we got the transmission packed, and I sat in the car and drank a Pepsi while the guy worked on it, then we left but din't get the tire fixed so we went to the other one, whether it was Tate's or Dale's, where we got the rim fixed. There we got some bullets and gloves and more maps, and they had a burger joint I went in to buy us some hamburgers, and the woman in there was givin me nasty looks and I thought how bout we kill you too, you old hag? We just got our hamburgers and left though, and I caught Charlie makin eyes at that hussy behind the counter when we was leavin so I shoved him and he shoved me back, then we got in the car and et our hamburgers what tasted like dog food. I tole Charlie we should go back and shoot em in their face for serving garbage like that.

We din't have no plan yet and Charlie said you don't jump without havin a plan, that's the way it's done, so he said first fore we head out West we'd best go to Meyer's, Gus Meyer being this old coot Charlie knowed what had a farm and some land where Charlie liked to go hunt, and Charlie thought we'd go and camp out and figger up a plan so we drove on down to Meyer's place but the road was all muddy and slushy from the snow on Friday and as we went on it got worse and worse and the car was skiddin and slippin and finally it got stuck out by the old schoolhouse what been blown down by a tornado, where there was still a storm cellar down underground, where we killed Bob Jensen and Carol King, I stabbed that bitch in her nastiness good. That's what you get for messin with my man, you little hussy, that's what you get. I stabbed her in her nastiness where Charlie done it to her and I killed her again and again.

But that's later and you better wait for it, for now it was just us being stuck and trying to dig out the car, then we went and got in the cellar to try and warm up, and I tole Charlie I'd kill him myself if he didn't figger something out.

And he says, "Whyn't you kill me then?"

And I says, "Whyn't you figger something out?"

Then he tosses a gun at me and I catch it but almost drop it cuz its cold and hurts my hands and I say, ow you stupid shit, and Charlie says, "Why'nt you kill me, then, if you're gone do it?"

Well I gave him back the gun and said quit being a dummy. He snorted, then kicked the car tire, then said we'd best go ask Gus Meyer for help. So we walked down to Gus Meyer's and his dog was barking as we come up and he come out on the porch a see us and Charlie says we need help getting our car unstuck, then Meyer went back inside and Charlie went up the steps and shot him right in the back, and shot his dog too, but that dog he just winged and it run off. We done went in the house then, leaving the old man in the hallway, and I sat in the kitchen warming up while Charlie went around ransackin the place cuz he said Meyer had a bunch of money hidden somewhere, but then all he come back with was two guns and a hunnerd dollars and a jacket and two pairs a socks and two pairs a gloves.

I ast him "What you doing with two pairs a socks, you dummy?"

"I got one for you and one for me" he says.

"I don't need no dead man's socks" I tell him.

"Well I ain't gone pass up some nice new socks" he says "specially when the ones I got are half rotted."

Then he set right down and put that old man's socks on, both pairs one over the other, on account of it being cold he says. I just shook my head. A hunnerd dollars is one thing but a pair of socks is pretty mean to go stealin from a dead man. Then Charlie says how he's hungry so he gets up and looks in the fridge, what din't have much in it but some Jell-O, so he et some Jell-O and some cookies he found and I had some too, then we went upstairs and took a nap.

Charlie been thinkin a that dog he shot, Meyer's dog, and how it gone off all wounded, and he said we better go fine it or somebody a know something was wrong at old Meyer's. So I sighed and tole him he always thought of stuff when it's too late, like maybe oncet he could come up with a plan ahead a time maybe, and he said "You din't do much better, Miss Know-It-All" and I says "Pshaw. I ain't the one goin around shootin people's dogs."

"Well, let's go fine it" he said, so we went out and all up through the mud lookin for this dog, and we found it out in the old man's pasture and it was lying on its side breathing shallow, bleeding and just lying there, its ribs coming up and down, the hole where Charlie shot it dark red and chunky, just like the Jell-O he et. I said "Charlie you better shoot him" and he says "That dog's already dead" so we stood there for a minute lookin at it in the cold, then turned around and went back to the house. Charlie covered Meyer up with a blanket and collected all his loot, then we went back to the car up the muddy road.

I think when you tell somebody a story you oughtn't to stop and say how the sky was so-and-so, or the flowers were gold and blue and wavin all in the wind, you oughta just get on with it and say what happened and who to, but there's times when what it looked like is just what it was and you can't know nothing about it unless you see it, and that day in Nebraska was a cold January day with thin blue light all across the sky and the earth muddy brown and gray, dirt all mixed with snow and ice and old rotted wheat, and out where we was the flat just went on forever like you was in a frozen white sea dirty with the floating bits and bobs of a wrecked old sailin ship. In the wintertime you look at Nebraska and it's sure enough the loneliest, most godforsaken spot on earth, like there ain't nobody lives there and nobody in a right mind who'd want to.

Anyways, Charlie and me went back to his car and worked it and after a couple hours we finally got it outta the rut but Charlie that dummy stripped the reverse gear getting it out. Then we drove back out to the road but Charlie was talking to me about what the police would do when they found out, like what he knowed from shows about how they did their dragnets, and he weren't paying attention to the road and just at the spot where Meyer's lane hit the main road Charlie durned stuck the car again. And I says "Charlie Starkweather, I swear you're the worse driver I ever seen."

"I'll show you some driving" he said. "It's this durnd mud."

So we got out and was trying to unstick the car again, which was near impossible this time on account a him strippin the reverse, then a farmer pulls up in his Ford truck and asks us if we need help and we says yes, so he tows us outta the ditch and Charlie gives him two dollars and says thanks, mister, then we get back in the car. So Charlie just sat there for a minute and I says "What?" And he says "I think maybe we just lay low at Meyer's for a couple days."

Well I says "I don't like being in there with that dead old man in the hallway."

"I'll haul him out to the yard if you want" he tells me. "I just think if the police are after us then it's best we lay low for a couple days."

But I ask him can't we go to Washington or Montana?

"We will" he says, and I shoulda known better he was lying to me, the dirty sumbitch, "but I think it's best if we hole up somewheres for a couple days and wait out the search, so's they don't catch us on the highway. Then we can go, after all the noise dies down."

"Let's go then" I says, so we drove back down the lane to Meyer's place and made it all the way this time without getting stuck at all on account a Charlie being real careful. Oncet we got there, though, we got outta the car and walked up and Charlie looked in the window in the door and saw how the blanket he put on the old man weren't there no more, and he turned right around and said "We gotta go" and I says "How come?" and he says "They knowed we was here" and I felt a fright go through me like the shivers and we got in the car and drove right off. He said he knowed a shortcut to Tate's where we could go and fix the transmission so we head off down another dirt road and I ask him what he saw and he says "Somebody took the blanket off him" and I thought that's smart, there, catching that. I din't want to stay there anyway. I had a bad feeling about the place and I told him so.

Turned out his shortcut weren't no shortcut at all but a dead end, so he circled round in a field and headed back out the road and we drove out to Tate's. The man on at Tate's said he couldn't fix the reverse less we left it till tomorrow, so we just bought some more bullets and another map. We got back in the car and Charlie says to me "I was thinking about the Meyer place and I's thinking maybe it's the wind blew off that blanket. I don't think nobody been there. I think it's the wind."

"I don't want to go back there, Charlie" I tole him.

And he says "I tole you we should hole up somewheres. It's the best place to do it, and we can lay low till the dragnet passes. And I think it's just the wind what blowed that blanket off. Ain't nobody been there."

"I don't think that's a good idea" I says.

"You're just scared of the dead body" he says "and we gotta hole up. We don't wanna get caught in no dragnet."

So I frowned at him, so's he'd know I didn't think it's such a good idea, but as we went on and got closer and closer

down the muddy lane the thought of what we'd find there
got worser and worser for me, till finally I saw how there'd
be police and ghosts and my parents all waiting for us, waiting to catch us down and I says "Charlie, stop. We can't go.
I got a premonition."

"A what?" he says.

"A premonition a evil" I tole him. "We can't go there or
that's it."

"What kind a premonition?"

"A premonition a evil! I sense danger. We gotta go on to
Montana, Charlie. I can feel it."

He stopped the car and set there looking at the sky getting dark and hunched over the wheel thinking, and finally
he saw things my way and turned around in the field, but
when we come back onto the road Charlie hit a ditch and
stuck the car again. He cursed and hit the steering wheel.

"There's your premonition right there!" he says.

"At least we're close to the road" I says "so's we can get a
ride."

"What'll we do with a ride?" he shouts at me. "Ain't
nowheres they can take us!"

"Ain't you a outlaw yet, Charlie Starkweather?" I says. I's
starting a get angry. "You a outlaw by true, you best start
thinking like one. We kill em and we take their car. We
take what we want, Charlie Starkweather. Don't you know
you're free? You're a free man now, a free white American,
you better start acting like it."

"You're right" he says, nodding his head. "You're right.
We'll hitch up a ride then bang, I'll just shoot em and take
their car. I love you, Caril."

"I love you, Charlie."

So we took our knives and a couple guns and I took my red swim bag and we walked out to the road and it was getting dark so we waited and waited and finally it was dark and then a big old Chevrolet come up and the man driving it was a big, fatheaded square with his Miss Priss girlfriend, and she give us a dirty look but the feller said "You need a ride?" and Charlie said "Sure nuff and yes we do."

We got in the back and the feller tried to help Charlie with the rifle what was wrapped up in a blanket but Charlie tole him I got it. The feller introduced hisself as Bob Jensen and his snotty little Miss Priss was Carol King, and we said we was Charlie Starkweather and Caril Fugate. Bob knowed Charlie from somewheres and they got to talking about cars for a minute then he ast where we was going. Charlie said we just needed to call somebody to come pick us up, so Bob said he'd take us into Bennet where he knowed a service station with a phone. We got there and the station was closed, and Bob said he knowed the guy who lived in back of the station and was gonna go get him up so Charlie could use the phone but then Charlie put his rifle against the back of his big fat stupid head and said "I don't think we need no phone, Bob. I think you're gone drive us all the way to Lincoln, then we're getting on State Highway 2."

"You're not gonna kill us are you?" Bob Jensen ast all scared-like.

"I ain't gonna kill you unless you try something stupid" Charlie said. "So let's just go get it done."

So then Bob pulled out the station and headed back toward Lincoln. It was electric in the car and I got a feeling

of what it must a been like for Charlie when he killed Bob
Colvert, it was like we had power over them and they was
scared of us and in our mercy. It weren't like when we killed
Ma and Marion, or like when he shot ol Gus Meyer, but it
was something tickly and wonderful how they kept looking back at us, frowning and acting like whupped dogs,
and it was like if we told em boo they'd sure as heck pee
theyselves. Now I knowed what it was like to have a power
over somebody, and have them be bossed at for a while, and
when they tried to talk up some kinda way out, Charlie
tole em just drive. We headed back towards Lincoln but
then Charlie changed his mind and had them drive back at
the Meyer place. "You know that ol blown-down school by the
Meyer place?" he says, and fathead says "Yes I do," so Charlie
says "That's where we're goin'."

"But there ain't nothing there" fathead says. "You ain't
gonna kill us are you?"

"No, I ain't" says Charlie, winking at me, "I just gotta
put you somewheres so we can head off fore you go to the
police."

"We wouldn't go to the police" fathead says.

"You must think I'm pretty stupid to believe that load a
pucky. How bout you just drive?"

Then I says, "Charlie, we forgot a take their money."

And he says that's right, and he tole em to give over whatever money they had.

"Why don't you leave us alone?" the girl cried, like a little
baby, and I grabbed her by the hair and said "I'll kill you
myself, bitch! You just do what we tell you!"

Eventually we got out to the old school and parked and

Charlie had them get outta the car and then he got out and covered em with his rifle and marched em over to the cellar. I stayed in the car waitin, watchin em go down. He sent the girl down first, then ol fathead, then just after fathead started goin down Charlie shot him, over and over, I member it was like ten times cuz I counted. I saw him there standin in the headlights at the mouth of the cellar, shootin down into it like he's shootin rats. Then he went down in the cellar and I set and waited. I thought he was gon shoot that hussy right off, but oncet I set there for a minute I realized he must a been doin somethin else, and then I figgered out what he must a been doin so I got out and went and shouted down "Charlie!" and then I shouted again. He shouted back "What?" and I shouted down "Come up here!" and then a minute later he come up the stairs with his gun and said "What?"

"I'll kill you right now, you dirty no good runt, I'll kill you my own self."

"What are you talking about?"

"I know what you're doin down there."

"No, it ain't what you think. I ain't done nothin."

"Charlie Starkweather, I'm giving you two minutes to go down there and kill that hussy or I'm gonna drive off and tell the police what you done."

"No, look darling, it's too cold to do anything. Look, I ain't—"

But I knowed he's lyin so I says "You kill her right now, or else" then I got back in the car, this time in the driver's seat. He shook his head at me then went back down the steps then I heard his gun go off and seed him coming

back up the steps. When he got back I shifted over in the
seat and he got in and asks me if I's happy and I says yes.
Then he tried to get out but the car was stuck, and he
cursed and hit the wheel. We both got outta the car and I
couldn't stop thinkin of that little hussy in the cellar and
of Charlie getting his wick all in her and I just kep getting
madder and madder, so while he was working on getting the
car unstuck I took my knife and went down and made
sure she was dead. First I pulled her dress up to see if she
had Charlie's milk all on her, which she din't, but she din't
have no panties on neither so I knowed what he done,
the little egg-sucker, and then thinking of it I got so mad
I just stabbed her in her nastiness all over, stabbing her
again and again and again till I was sure, then I went back
up and stood by the cellar stairs looking at Charlie trying
to get the car out. Eventerlly he did and we drove off.
Charlie and me didn't talk, cause I's mad at him and he
din't know what to say, he just looked at my bloody knife
and hands what I tried to wipe off on that girl's dress and
din't say nothing. So he was headed back to Lincoln
and oncet I realized, I said "What are you doin going back
to Lincoln?" and he said "We ain't got no food or nothing
and we need somewheres to sleep." So I said huh you must
be stupid, which showed true just as soon as we was back
in Lincoln when we drove by my old house, which Charlie wanted to see again, and there was police cars in front
and all over. So we drove on and then headed west out of
town. Back on the road Charlie said he thought we'd go
out West a ways and outrun their dragnet, and I said how
bout that, and then he put his hand on my knee and said

we had time for a little go, we could just pull over and have a little one, and I took his hand away and said "You already got yours today, Charlie Starkweather."

We drove west and west on the highway, not hardly talking, me thinking how nice it was to finally be rolling down the highway going somewheres and finally outta the mess behind us and we could finally start over, then I started getting sleepy so I went a sleep there with Charlie still driving, then I woke up later and saw a sign said LINCOLN.

"That's funny" I says.

"What?" he ast.

"That sign says LINCOLN."

"I had a idea" Charlie said. "I knowed this rich ol man, Mr. Ward, he lives in town and he got a whole bunch a money saved up that'd get us all the way to Washington State and get us a house too maybe, and I thought we go back and just take it. I knowed him from Donny's route, when I was haulin garbage, in the country-club part of town. Then I thought we can't go back to town cause the police are looking for us. But then I realized that's the last place they'd look. The police are gonna be going from Lincoln, looking for somebody leaving, they ain't gonna be looking for nobody coming back! Soon as I figured that out, I figured we orta head back and relieve ol Mr. Ward of his moneys."

And oncet I thought about it, that idea seemed pretty good to me, so I just went back to sleep until Charlie woke me up again saying we're here and I said what time is it and he said 3:40 in the A.M. We parked on a side street in town and went to sleep and didn't get up till after the sun come up. Then we drove to the ol Ward place and pulled in the driveway and Charlie said "Wait here till I signal" then went in with his gun. A few minutes later he waved me in and I went in the house. I tell you the truth, I never seen a kitchen so nice. They had a new icebox and lovely little dishes and all kinds a nice things, and Charlie was standing over two old women sitting at the table, and he said this here's Mrs. Clara Ward and this here's Lillian the maid, who's deaf but she can read your lips, he says. I thought about that later, how it must be like reading lips, like how do you know it's one word and not the other? Then I thought how if people can read lips they must be able to read eyes and faces and all of it, like it's not even words you say just words you think, just there on your face and in the air like it weren't even had to be said. There was a retriever too named Queenie and Mrs. Clara had a poodle lapdog named Suzy. I petted Queenie and sat down in a chair with the old women and said "Now what?"

Charlie set hisself down and said "We gone wait for Mr. Ward to come home so he can undo the safe and get us all the money we need. Why'nt you two women do some cleaning or something while we listen to the radio?" So we set there listening to the radio while the women did some cleaning, then Charlie left me with a gun to watch em and he poked around the house some, then a little later Charlie had Mrs. Ward make him some pancakes. Then when she made the pancakes he said "These pancakes taste like horse pucky. Make me some waffles." Then she made us some waffles and we et em. I told Charlie I was tired and wanted a go to sleep but he said we had to stay up to watch the women and I said why don't we just tie em up? Then he said we had to keep watch for Mr. Ward cuz we din't know when he was comin back. So we just set there and listened to the radio and the old women set there and ever so often they'd try to talk to us but me or Charlie'd tell em to shut your faces. What was one good thing was that they had the papers and we was *all over* them papers from killing Ma and Marion, so we went through and clipped out all the times they had us, looking for fugitive nineteen years old Charlie Starkweather, COLD-BLOODED KILLER, and his kidnap girlfriend Caril Ann Fugate, and how he was a KILLER ON THE LOOSE. They even had stories about ol Meyer being killed and fathead and his girlfriend gone missing. They was right behind us, we realized, and it's a good thing we come back to town like Charlie thought cuz now we done stymied their expectations. We thought it was all real funny but then when Mrs. Clara said "I think it's awful" I turned at her and showed her my knife and said "How'd you like me to stab you in your nastiness, you old hag?" and that shut her right up. We also wrote a letter "For the Law Only" explaining what we done, and discussed whether to leave it at the scene of the crime. A little later Mrs. Clara tole Charlie she needed to go upstairs a change her shoes and when she went up there she was gone for a while and after almost a hour I tole Charlie you better go find her. He did then I heard a gunshot and a scuffle and what I thought was great was how when the gunshot went off that deaf maid din't even look up—she really couldn't hear a thing! She just kept working on her knitting like it weren't nothing. It must be strange a be deaf, like you's at the bottom of the ocean or in a cave all the time, not being able to hear people, walking around like a secret.

Well anyways Charlie come back down and says she tried to shoot him so he had to stab her. He stood where the maid couldn't see his lips so she wouldn't know and he said don't tell her or she'll go crazy. Then he handed me the gun and went back upstairs with his bloody knife. He's up there for a while and I knowed what he was doin. I figgered that's what he's like now, I guess, no better'n a wild animal, and there weren't no changing him. He come back down later and said he done tied her up on the bed and left her there, and I said I bet you did, and he said for me to stay there while he moved the cars outside for when ol Ward came home. After he done that we set for a while readin the papers and jokin about how stupid everone was. Then Charlie looks over at me and says you know darling there's a chance we might not make it out alive.

"We'll make it out to Washington just like you said" I tole him.

"It might be a hail a bullets for us, darling. We should think on that. It may be we ain't maybe gonna make it out alive. But I say one thing: a man don't ask no greater glory till life is through than to spend one last minute in the wilderness."

I sushed him then and tole him quit being a dummy, but I thought he might just mean it, maybe he means for us to not make it, then I thought that's dumb. I din't know what but I thought we'd make it to Montana at least.

Anyways, after that, I said I'd go upstairs for him and wash the blood off the knife he left up there, so I went and got the knife and saw old lady Ward tied to that bed up there, bleedin slow and passed out, her face all white

and doughy and wet, and I got a sense a what Charlie
must a done, pulling up her old lady's dress and giving it
to her, I could see him rutting hisself in between her spin-
dly old knobby legs, and I walked up and felt her dress
myself and looked at her saggy old skin and face and then
I thought you little sumbitch you gon just keep stickin it
in everwhere you can so I stabbed her in the neck and in
her floppy old-lady udders, just stabbin and stabbin. It's
hard when you stab a body in the chest cuz the knife gets
up against the ribs there, but I kep goin and getting blood
all over, then I got tired so I left her there. Fore I left
I thought the room smelled awful a blood so I sprayed
some a her perfume on her. I washed the knife up and
my hands too in the bathroom and took it back downstairs and gave it to Charlie and said "You got yours and
I got mine." He din't know what I's talkin about and he's
thinking of his plans for getting ol man Ward, so he tells
me all about his big sheriff plan and how he wants me to
go wait in the dining room and give a holler when the old
man drives up so that's what I done. I curled up with a
blanket in the dining room and kep a eye on the window
and then by an by his car rolls up so I holler. I stay there
in the dining room like I'm a supposed to and I hear
Charlie and the Ward man talkin in the other room, then
there's a scuffle and some fightin, then I hear somebody
fall down the stairs into the cellar and a gun goes off, and
I think, I sure hope that's Charlie, but to be honest I din't
know if I hoped it was Charlie doing the shootin or Charlie the one who got shot. I loved him true, but things
were turnin funny and I thought if somebody din't kill

him soon I might have to, waitin up in the night maybe
while he slept and stabbin him in the throat, but then I
heard some steps and another gunshot, then some more
steps, and the old man bangs through the door heading for
the front, stumbling kinda and looking scared, and Charlie bangs through behin him and just as the old man gets
the front door Charlie plugs him again, bang, I remember the sparks coming out the rifle against the china hutch
where he was standing like a snapper on the Fourth of July
and the old man stumbled and leaned against the door and
fell down. Charlie looked at me and got out his knife and
said "Go get that deaf maid in the kitchen" then he went
over to finish off old man Ward. I got up like he said and
went into the kitchen but there weren't no maid. The back
door was still closed so I thought she must a gone down the
cellar. The light was on down there but I couldn't see her, so
I shouted for her to come up then I membered she was deaf.
I'd a gone down there but I thought she might have a gun
or something, which is what I tole Charlie when he come
back into the kitchen and started washing the blood off his
knife. So we set and waited for her and after a bit we saw
her at the bottom of the stairs and she din't have no gun or
nothin, and Charlie went down and got her, then me and
him took her upstairs and tied her to a bed.

"We don't need a kill her," Charlie says, "she's just some
deaf old maid."

Then he went down to load up the car and I looked at
the maid, who looked back at me all terrified, and I took
out my knife and showed it to her so she'd know I's serious. I weren't gone do nothin to her till I thought about

why Charlie wanted to keep her alive, and maybe it's cuz he din't get his fill with the old lady, and I thought, well he ain't gon do nothin if she's dead and she don't deserve to live anyway, hidin from us like a animal, what good's it being alive if you're deaf anyway? Sometimes I think you got a deaf baby or a blind one or something dumb or crippled you oughta just kill it right away, cuz the world's a hard-enough place as it is without addin to our troubles with being deaf or blind or crippled. So I got up and took a pillow and put it on her face so Charlie wouldn't hear if she screamed, and I was right cuz she started screaming right away, and I stabbed her in her fat belly and I cut up her arms and legs and stabbed her in her fat old udders too, stupid bitch with her old nag face deserved to die a hunnerd times and I stabbed her and stabbed her. After I was done I washed off again, feeling good about things being takin care of, then went downstairs and saw Charlie had black goo all in his hair and I said what you do to your head and he says "Shoe polish." "Well, that's dumb" I said. Then he ast me what that noise was and I tole him "That maid din't wanna die for nothing." Then he ast me why I done killed her and I said "Why I done it? Why *you* done it? Why you done it with that old hag? Why you done it to Ma and Marion? Why you done anything? You're a dirty sumbitch, Charlie Starkweather, and I ain't never seen no pot call no kettle black. Why you done it? Why I ain't done *you* yet, that's the question." Then he snorted and said do it if you're gonna, but I saw we had some more stuff to load in the car so I just said "Let's get outta here fore the police come by." And we did finally and Charlie said he wanted to see the house one more time so we drove by my house and there was a light on in the kitchen and a police car in the driveway and that felt funny, I thought what it must a been like for a lonely policeman standin in our kitchen or maybe eatin cold chicken and drinkin a beer at our table, who knows, and was he waiting for us or just doin police work, like doin for evidence, and if he's waiting for us I thought for a moment it'd be just as well we obliged him, then we'd tie him up and find out what they knew then kill him too and it'd be one less policeman after us and we'd know their plans but I din't say nothin and Charlie got the willies so we just got back on the highway and headed west. We was driving awhile and Charlie tells me he's getting in the mood thinking about how beautiful I am and I tells him "You had yours for today," and he looked at me funny like he din't know what I was talking about and I said "Just keep drivin, mister. We got about a hunnerd police after us." Then we stopped for gas, and then we kept goin, drivin into the night like two lost stars crossin a endless sky. We went through Seward and York and Grand Island and Cairo and Ravenna and Hazard. We stopped at Broken Bow and got some more gas and maps, it musta been after midnight, and the whole place seemed as lonely as you could ever imagine. Charlie tole me he wrote a confession on the bathroom wall there but din't sign it, then we got back on the road and headed west again, goin through the Sand Hills, that's the farthest I ever been from home, and all those low grassy hills rolling across the world, covered with snow and ice and dead grass pokin up in the night and the stars twinklin down on us from the coalpile sky, the earth silver like a frozen sea, and I was sleepy and it was late but I finally felt like we got ourselves free a little, like we finally got away from Lincoln, and it was wonderful and scary, like the future was open before us with a darkness dark as a clouded night sky, and it was ours to make into whatever we wanted, like we could just dream it into happening and there weren't no police behind us and no parents tellin us what to do and no stupid school to go to, it was all just promise and wonderland and we'd have our cabin and babies and freedom and future. It felt like we could just start over. It was a beautiful night and a beautiful dream going into the night, then Charlie fell asleep and almost drove into a ditch and he waked up right away and pulled back onto the road and said "We should stop and sleep."

"We can't stop" I tole him "there's about a hunnerd cops after us and we gotta keep goin."

"I can't keep on" he said. "I'm too sleepy."

"Well, you gotta" I said.

"Maybe I could if we did some kissing" he said. "That'd keep me going for another couple hours."

"I tole you, you already got yours for today."

"You think I did that old lady?" he ast.

"I can't imagine what else you's doing up there so long."

"Hell I did," he says. "I ain't gone poke some old lady. C'mon, darling. Let's just make some love and I'll keep driving all night."

"Fine" I tole him, and I let him kiss me and I milked him off into some ol napkins, cuz with all we had goin on I din't need no babies on top of it. So then he drove on another five or ten minutes then pulled over and said "I'm just too tired," and I cursed him for being a lazy dog and a liar and a dirty sumbitch, but he just went to sleep and so did I.

In the morning fore we left Nebraska we stopped and got some more gas and candy bars for breakfast and nine bottles of Pepsi-Cola. It was a beautiful blue day showin all the promise of a dead world waitin to be reborn, and as we crossed the border into Wyomin with the sun lookin down on us I thought we surely would make it across and everthing was possible, but then I saw the mountains and it was the first time I seed em ever, all dark and high against the edge of the prairie and my heart dropped cuz I thought there weren't no way and I was sad and angry cuz I knowed they was after us, we heard all about us on the radio and Charlie says they knowed what kinda car we had, he says we gotta switch cars, so we stops at this Buick and then Charlie goes up and tells the guy open the door but he won't do it so Charlie done pull out his gun and shot him musta been ten times and then another man drives up and he gets out and Charlie points the gun at him but he grabs it then him and Charlie start rasslin and that's when the deputy drives up and I see my chance and run up to his car and say "Take me to the police" and he says "Get in the car" so I did and tells him how Charlie killed a man there and he asks me who that is and I just look at him all funny like don't you know? "That there's Charlie Starkweather."

Suzie put her pen down and closed the notebook. Abelard lay sleeping on the bed. She took off her glasses and rubbed her eyes, closed the drapes, then got up to brush her teeth. She had a lot of driving to do to in the morning, through the pass over the mountains, and the forecast called for strange weather.

Maybe tomorrow she'd start over. Maybe tomorrow he'd let her go.

ACKNOWLEDGMENTS

I'm consistently delighted and grateful that I get to work with Mark Doten, and I appreciate to no end his help on this unusual book. Most of all, I appreciate the willingness he and Soho Press continue to show for publishing and supporting innovative work. I'm not only grateful to them for giving my own work a home, but proud to be part of their larger effort.

Deep thanks to Patrick Blanchfield, Travis Just, Hilary Plum, Sharon Mesmer, Jake Siegel, and Martin Woessner for reading versions or pieces of this book and talking with me about them.

The inspirations and influences that provoked and inflected this novel are too numerous to list, but a few of the most important ones can and should be named: Jean-Luc Godard's *Weekend* (1967); Tom Waits's *Bone Machine* (1992); Toni Morrison's *Playing in the Dark: Whiteness and the Literary Imagination* (1993); Dave Lapham's *Stray Bullets* series (1995–present); the work of Irish composer Jennifer Walshe (especially *XXX_LIVE_NUDE_GIRLS!!!* [2003] and *Motel Abandon* [2005]); Object Collection's opera *Problem Radical(s)* (2009); Professor Tamsen Wolff's course on the twentieth-century American musical, for which I was lucky enough to be a teaching assistant while at Princeton; the music of *Tyrants*; and Daniel Fish's revisionist 2015 production of *Oklahoma!* Similarly, detailing all the books, films, songs, and disjecta membra folded into this novel as research, discursive texture, and raw material for collage would be a thankless and tedious task, but a handful of the most important sources should be cited, including William Allen, *Starkweather: Inside the Mind of a Teenage Killer*, Clerisy Press, 2004; Ninette Beaver, B. K. Ripley, and Patrick Trese, *Caril*, Lipincott, 1974; Jeff O'Donnell, *Starkweather: A Story of Mass Murder on the Great Plains*, J&L Lee, 1993; Julia Adeney Thomas, "History and Biology in the Anthropocene: Problems of Scale, Problems of Value," *American Historical Review*, 119:5 (December 1, 2014), 1587–1607; and Walt Whitman, "Starting from Paumanok," from *Leaves of Grass,* 1881.

I would also like to offer my gratitude to the Lannan Foundation and the University of Notre Dame for their material support in making this work possible.

At last, for Sara, my first, best reader, my perennial road-trip companion, my life and breath, and for Reyzl, who has made the old roads new and strange again, who brightens the gloomy horizon with joy—thank you.